Keys to the City

ALSO BY LISA SCHROEDER

My Secret Guide to Paris
Sealed with a Secret

Charmed Life:
#1: *Caitlin's Lucky Charm*
#2: *Mia's Golden Bird*
#3: *Libby's Sweet Surprise*
#4: *Hannah's Bright Star*

It's Raining Cupcakes
Sprinkles and Secrets
Frosting and Friendship

Keys to the City

*LISA SCHROEDER

SCHOLASTIC PRESS | NEW YORK

WITHDRAWN

All rights reserved. Published by Scholastic Press, an imprint of Scholastic Inc., *Publishers since 1920.* SCHOLASTIC, SCHOLASTIC PRESS, and associated logos are trademarks and/or registered trademarks of Scholastic Inc.

Library of Congress Cataloging-in-Publication Data available
ISBN 978-0-545-90738-5

10 9 8 7 6 5 4 3 2 1   17 18 19 20 21

Printed in the U.S.A.   23
First edition, June 2017
Book design by Yaffa Jaskoll

For one of my amazing
high school English teachers,
Mrs. Phillips,
and her granddaughter Eva~
I'm so grateful for your support.

PS: PUBLIC SCHOOL

This is what summer should be: fun family picnics, ice cream cones, trips to the beach, pool time, curling up with a good book, and more ice cream.

This is what summer should *not* be: a school project in the form of an acronym.

Our middle school principal, Mrs. Lindenberg, is the queen of acronyms. Like a lot of people, I love DEAR: Drop Everything And Read. But at our school, simply one acronym is not enough. In PE, BEE stands for Best Effort is Expected. Ms. Frindle, the PE teacher, occasionally tells us we aren't being very good bees, even though we aren't bees, we're kids. Isn't that kind of weird? Why doesn't she just tell us to try harder, if that's what she means?

And in the cafeteria, there's FAVE, which means Fruits And Veggies Every day. "Make sure you've got your fave," the lunch lady will tell us. Would it really be so hard to add a few syllables on and just say "fruits and veggies"? I don't get it.

So when Mrs. Lindenberg told us at our end-of-year seventh-grade assembly that she had a new acronym for us, it did not make us excited.

"Are you ready for it?" she asked as she looked at us over her reading glasses, her brown hair piled into a high bun on top of her head, like always. Maybe she expected us to cheer or something, but the auditorium stayed quiet. "It's really fun, and it's going to make this summer unforgettable for you." Sorry, Mrs. Lindenberg, but unless it's the latest iPhone you're handing out, getting seventh graders excited is not easy.

I looked over at my friends Nora and Talia. They shrugged. I shrugged back.

When Mrs. Lindenberg didn't get the response she expected, she cleared her throat and looked down at her notes on the podium. "Your new acronym is HAT, and this summer you, dear seventh graders, are going to try on different hats and see which ones fit the best. Metaphorically speaking, of course."

With the microphone in hand, she went to the large whiteboard that had been wheeled onto the stage earlier and wrote:

Heart

Abilities

Talent

Then she underlined each of the words as she talked. "Follow your *heart* to discover your *abilities* and *talents*. In other words, use this summer to explore your interests. Through that process, my hope is that you will discover where your abilities and talents might lie. Please understand, this does not mean you have to be proficient at something by the end of the summer. The goal is to simply discover one or two things you'd like to focus on in the near future. You see, it's important to know what your HAT looks like so that next year you can apply for the right high schools for *you*. It's a very personal decision, and that's why this project is a personal one as well.

"There are no guidelines, really, but I want you to think big! Get creative. The sky is the limit here, okay? Your first graded assignment, as eighth graders, will be a poster you make and bring the first week. Show us what excites you, what moves you, or what you learned about yourself on this journey of the heart. We'll fill the hallways with your discoveries! Imagine how motivational that will be as you start your new year. You can draw or paint, you can make a collage, you can show us in words—whatever works best for you. Does everyone understand your assignment?"

Some kids nodded their heads. Others said, "Mm-hmm." I wanted to cry out, "Don't do this to us, please!" But I stopped myself.

"Wonderful," she said. "Now, to inspire you, I've invited three of our fabulous alumni to show you how they've gone on in life to make use of their talents and abilities. We'll hear a cello piece, watch a jazz dance routine, and see a science experiment in action. At this time, I'd like to invite onto the stage . . ."

I turned to Talia, who was sitting next to me, and whispered in her ear, "You're so lucky. You already know you love to dance. You're going to apply to that one performing arts high school you told us about, right?"

She whispered back, "Yeah. But it's not a sure thing."

Still, I thought to myself, she *knew*. I wanted some of that knowing.

I turned my attention back to the stage as a young woman sat on a chair with her cello in front of her and raised her bow to begin playing. The only instrument I knew how to play, and not very well, was the ukulele. Dad liked to "jam" with me sometimes—that's what he called it, anyway. What a joke. Obviously. I wasn't very good, but it was fun to play with him. I'd never play outside of my house, though. Way too embarrassing. And other instruments didn't really interest me.

What else was there? Summer hadn't even started, and I felt anxious and frustrated with this project already.

As the sad cello music floated through the auditorium, I reached into the pocket of my jacket and pulled out my little notebook covered with tiny, colorful hedgehogs. For some reason, when I felt anxious, writing helped me. So I decided that's what I would do while keeping half an eye on the stage.

The notebook had been one of things I'd bought with the money I received in my red envelope from my grandmother for Chinese New Year. Although my adoptive family is not Chinese, we still celebrate the holiday with a party and gifts. They think it's important to honor my heritage, and I love them for that.

Since the day I'd brought home the notebook, I'd written something in it practically every day. At first, I treated it more like a journal but that got boring, so I started doing other kinds of writing—poems and short stories mostly. I'd even sent in a story to a magazine our librarian had mentioned to our language arts class one day. She'd told us that very few magazines take story submissions from kids, but this one did. So without really thinking, I typed up my story and sent it in. But I hadn't received a response. Every time I thought about someone getting my silly little story in the mail, reading it, and hating it so much they couldn't even send me a letter back, I felt kind of sick to my stomach.

From now on, I'd decided, my writing, like my ukulele playing, would not be shared with the outside world. That way it would stay fun, and I didn't have to worry about embarrassing myself ever again.

The cello solo ended, and everyone applauded.

Nora leaned in and said to Talia and me, "I loved that *so* much, I think I want to play the cello."

I gave her a funny look. "Really? That was fast."

She grinned. "It was so beautiful! I've never heard one before. Maybe when you know, you know? I'm going to ask my parents if I can rent one this summer. Think they'll let me take some lessons?"

"Probably," I said.

"Do you want to try it, too?" she asked me.

I wanted to say yes. I wanted to have it be that easy. But the truth was, I wanted to play the cello about as much as I wanted to give an assigned speech in humanities the following week. "I don't think so," I said. "But thanks for asking."

As Mrs. Lindenberg introduced the next person who

would be performing, Talia whispered, "You'll find your thing, Lindy. Don't worry."

Hopefully she was right. Still, why did I have a feeling it was going to be a LONG (Look Out Nothing Good is going to happen) summer?

Summertime

A poem by Lindy Mackay

Fresh lemonade.
Golden sun.
Swimming suits.
Family fun.
Purple Popsicles.
Suntan lotion.
Library visits.
Baseball in motion.

(Here I thought the only hat I'd have to worry about
this summer was which one to wear to a Mets game.)

Chapter 2

BOROUGH: BIGGER THAN A NEIGHBORHOOD,

SMALLER THAN A CITY

Two days later, on Sunday afternoon, Nora and I walked in front of our mothers, just far enough so they couldn't listen in on our conversation.

"Do you think good dancers are born that way?" I asked Nora.

It was a pretty Sunday in Brooklyn, with a bright blue sky above us as we made our way toward the subway. We'd just come from watching Talia perform a ballet piece at her studio's spring showcase, and it had been amazing.

"Nope," Nora said. "You know how much Talia

practices. And even when we're messing around at the park or whatever, she's always twirling around."

"But maybe she came out that way," I argued.

Nora laughed. "Pretty sure babies don't twirl, Lindy. They cry. They sleep. They poop. But they don't twirl. Why are you thinking about this?"

I shrugged. "It's something I've always wondered about. When someone is talented, like Talia or her idol, Misty Copeland, where does the talent come from? Like, why don't I have that kind of talent?"

"You could take ballet, you know," Nora said. "Just like Mrs. Lindenberg said, it's never too late to try something new."

"But I don't want to take ballet. I wouldn't be good at it."

"How do you know?"

In my black pants and red shoes, I stopped and stuck my right leg behind me, trying to do an arabesque. I turned my head, my straight black hair falling in front of my face, and my standing leg wobbled. I couldn't even hold the position standing still. I was about as graceful as a horse on roller skates.

"See?" I said as I put both feet back on the sidewalk. "Okay, here are the things I know for sure I'm good at. Eating doughnuts. Choosing just the right emoji for a text. And finding the perfect book to check out at the library. Do you think any of those will work for my HAT project?"

Nora laughed. "Emojis? Really?"

"Hey, it's not as easy as it seems. Pick the wrong face and you might offend someone. Like, I'm pretty sure you only want to use that red-faced, I'm-really-mad one in rare situations."

"Lindy?"

"Yes?"

"You should see if a comedy club would let you perform."

"Um, I'm really not that funny."

"I think you are. And with some practice, you'd get even funnier. I feel like you have what it takes to get up on stage and make people laugh."

"Okay, so if I did that, then what? Sit back and watch all the high schools fight over the funny Asian girl? I doubt that."

"But that's the thing. I bet they'd love you because you'd stand out."

I groaned. "Why do we have to stand out? I just want to be me. Quiet, book-loving me."

"Yes, but we're supposed to follow our hearts and reach for the sky!"

"You're lucky, Nora. If the cello thing doesn't work out, you still have a unique talent."

She stared at me. "I do?"

"Yes! You're like a walking, talking Paris travel guide. You love Paris, right? The same way Talia loves ballet."

We stopped at the subway station and waited for our moms to catch up. "Huh," she said. "I guess you're right. Mom did mention something to me about a French immersion high school."

"See?" I said. "You already have two possibilities for your HAT project, which is two more than I have at the moment."

"You have all summer," she said. "And I can help you if you want. Even though it would be much easier if you still lived in the same neighborhood, and not all the way over in Manhattan."

"I know. But the good news is, Mom told me you can sleep over pretty soon. We've just been so busy getting everything ready for the B&B's grand opening coming up next weekend."

Nora looked at her mom when she approached. "Can we go to their grand opening? Please?"

"Of course we can," Faye, Nora's mother, said. "I can't wait to see the place."

Nora and I beamed at each other—she could finally see my new room, up close and personal. She'd helped me make every decorating decision along the way, like best friends do.

When I had showed her a picture of the bedspread I'd picked out, she'd said, "You know what would go really well that?"

"What?"

"Butterflies." I'd looked at her, confused. "Find a butterfly stencil. Paint butterflies on the wall. It'll be *so* cute."

She knew I had a thing for the fluttery little creatures. I did a report on the migration of the monarch butterflies last year, and I'd talked about them almost nonstop for an entire month.

So I'd done as she suggested with one of the walls in my room. And she was exactly right. I told her she should start a design show for teens. HGTV would be lucky to have her. I was starting to think there wasn't anything my best friend couldn't do.

Now, as I turned to say good-bye, I tried not to feel a little jealous of Nora.

"See you at school tomorrow, Lindy. Our last week before freedom!"

"Freedom with a HAT on its head," I called out as I headed down the stairs after my mother to take the subway back to Greenwich Village. "Hey, if you get bored later, text me!"

"And you'll reply with the perfect emojis?" she replied.

I laughed. "Of course! It's my specialty, remember?"

A Friendship for All Seasons

A limerick by Lindy Mackay

There once was a girl named Lindy,
who met her best friend in kindy.
They'd run and they'd skip
and were glued at the hip,
even when it was rainy and windy!

Chapter 3

BROWNSTONE: A TALL, NARROW TOWNHOUSE WITH A BROWN STONE FACADE

The train ride back to our new neighborhood in Manhattan was just long enough to make up a limerick about Nora and me. I learned about limericks in fifth grade during our poetry unit. They're fun to write, but also kind of hard because you have to stick to a certain rhythm while at the same time finding words that rhyme with each other. It's easiest if you pick a word in the first line that rhymes with lots of other words. I could only think of two words that rhyme with Lindy, so I had to figure out a way to use both of them.

"This is our stop," Mom reminded me. By now I

knew that, but she probably just wanted to make sure. With our old apartment, she never had to tell me. At least as far back as I could remember. Both Mom and Dad had said it would take time to get used to everything about living at the new place, and that it was normal to miss my old home.

It had always been my parents' dream to own a bed-and-breakfast. They'd taken out a loan and bought the 1880 brownstone over a year ago, and completely renovated the inside by replacing pipes, fixtures, and wiring, updating the kitchen, repairing walls and floors, and installing air-conditioning. During that time, my mom liked to drag me along with her to flea markets, where we'd look for "fabulous finds." At first, I had no idea what this meant. Then she explained that a fabulous find was a piece of vintage furniture that would look beautiful in the B&B but wouldn't cost an arm and a leg.

"So cheap but pretty?" I'd asked her.

"Basically, yes," she'd said.

I guess calling a vintage piece of furniture a fabulous find sounds better, though. Our flea market shopping paid off. Every room was now decorated like something out of a television show featuring a rich British family living in a hundred-year-old manor.

The brownstone had three floors of guest rooms plus the main floor with the library, a large dining room, and the kitchen. Our family lived on the fourth floor, in our own apartment, complete with a small kitchen, a family room, and three bedrooms. Although I missed my old neighborhood, I adored my new bedroom. I finally had just enough space for a bookcase. And when I ran out of room on mine, my mom said I could put books in the formal library downstairs as long as I was willing to share with kids who might want to read one while they were staying with us. I loved the idea of having a library in our home so much, how could I possibly mind sharing?

When we walked through the front door of our house, soon to also be known as the Chorus Inn, we found my brother about to slide down the elegant banister of the staircase.

"Davis!" my mom said. "What are you doing? This isn't a playground."

He jumped off and plastered on a big fake smile, walking the rest of the way down the steps. "Oh. Hi, Mom. Hi, Lindy. How was the ballet?"

My brother is ten years old and knows how to turn on the charm like a faucet. It's almost magical, the way he does it. I see through him almost every time, but my mother loves good manners, so whenever he does his politeness routine, she becomes spellbound. Like I said, magic.

"Oh, it was wonderful," Mom said. "Wasn't it, Lindy?

The theme was movies, and every age group danced to a song from a film. Like, Lindy's friend Talia chose *The Sound of Music*. How was your game?"

Prince Charming continued to smile. "Good. We won. Got home a little while ago. Dad's making dinner. I helped peel some carrots and potatoes."

Mom reached out and stroked his head of brown hair, which had lots of natural curl, like our dad's. "Thanks for doing that, buddy."

Years ago, they didn't think they could have any children, so they went to China and adopted me. Then, just as they were getting ready to start the process to adopt another baby, Mom found out she was pregnant. Surprise!

Sometimes I get a little bit jealous of Davis because he's their biological child. But Mom always tells me if she could choose any daughter in the world, one with their blood or not, they'd choose me every single time.

One time I had said, "But if you chose Taylor Swift, you'd be rich."

She'd laughed. "Melinda Jia Mackay, you think I'd rather be rich than have you as a daughter? What kind of shallow human being do you think I am?" She'd pulled me into her arms then. "I don't want Taylor Swift or anyone else. I want you. Always remember that."

The thing is, I think she really means it, so I guess I

18

have nothing to be upset about. It'd sure be nice if some people wouldn't look at us funny when we're all out together, though. It's like they forget a family doesn't have to look a certain way.

"Shall we all go up?" Mom asked. "I'll see what I can do to help Dad with dinner. Lindy, can you set the table, please?"

"Sure," I said as I started up the staircase with Mom and Davis trailing behind me. "But can I change first?"

"As long as you don't change into a shark," Davis said. "Hard to set the table with only fins."

Clearly, Nora was wrong. Davis should be a comedian, not me. "I just want to change out of these nice clothes, weirdo."

"Hey, now," Mom said. "No name-calling. And yes, honey, you may change."

When we reached our apartment at last (most beautiful old brownstones don't have elevators), we went our separate ways. I went into my room and shut the door. The blue-and-yellow combination I'd chosen still made me smile. My bed looked so soft, so inviting, I had to resist the urge to lie down and snuggle up with a book. I slipped my notebook and pen out of my pocket before I tossed my jacket onto the bed. Then I went over to the window with its built-in window seat and sat down.

I loved this time of year, when the sun stayed out a

long time. Before the HAT project, it felt like the summer had been laid out so nicely, like tea and scones at one of my favorite restaurants, Alice's Tea Cup. The inn was finished, we were all moved in, and so I'd imagined lots of fun times with my family and friends, and time by myself to read and write. But now? How was I supposed to figure out what I'm naturally talented at doing anyway? Some kids could look to their parents and get some hints. Like, hey, my dad is good at basketball, maybe I am, too. But that wouldn't work for me. I didn't know anything about my birth parents, although I sometimes wondered about them.

With a big sigh, I leaned back into the pillows and opened my notebook. I knew it wouldn't do any good to sit there and worry. So I decided to work on a story I'd started a few weeks ago.

Many Flowers, Many Families

A story by Lindy Mackay

A man went shopping for a flower bouquet to give to his mother for her birthday. Since the supermarket was close to his home, he went there, figuring it would be easiest. But when he got there, he discovered all the flower bouquets were the same.

Red roses, pink carnations, and white lilies.

He went to the clerk and said, "Don't you have anything else? My mother doesn't like carnations. Her favorite flower is the Gerber daisy. I was hoping for a bouquet of those."

She shrugged. "That's all we have. Can't you just pick the carnations out if she doesn't like them?"

"I guess I wanted something different," he said. "Something special. Why do you make only one bouquet, anyway?"

"It's easiest."

"But it's boring," the man said. "What if the bakery only sold one type of cake? What if the library only carried one type of book? What if—"

"Okay, okay," the clerk said. "I get your point. Look, I'll make your mother a bouquet with lots of roses and no carnations. How's that sound?"

He shook his head. "No, thanks. I'm going somewhere else. Like I said, I want a bouquet that is special. Because my mother is very, very special."

The clerk told him, "She's lucky to have you as a son."

"She never got married but wanted a son. She adopted me and raised me all by herself. Maybe our family doesn't look like most families, but it doesn't matter. She is my family, and I am hers. And a bouquet of daisies is still a lovely bouquet even if there isn't a rose in the bunch. See what I mean?"

"I suppose I do," the clerk said. Then he watched as she opened a notebook that said Flower Farms.

Maybe next time there will be a lot more flowers to choose from, he thought to himself.

And even though the man left the store without any flowers, he did leave with a smile on his face.

Chapter 4

TAKE THE TRAIN: TAKE THE SUBWAY (INTERCHANGEABLE)

There was a gentle knock at my door before it opened. "Lindy? It's been over twenty minutes. Can you please come set the table?"

I stashed my notebook underneath the cushion and jumped up. "Oh, yeah, sorry."

Over dinner, Mom and Dad talked about the grand opening scheduled for next weekend. They'd managed to get a reporter to run a small article in the *New York Times*, which they were both really excited about. Dad said news coverage was the best way to get the word out. Mom had also contacted some of the local television stations, but so far no one had gotten back to her.

"There's still time," she said. "We'll just have to wait and see."

"What happens at the grand opening?" Davis asked. "And can I have more roast, please?"

Mom passed the plate to him. "It's basically an open house. People will come in and take a look around. Your dad and I will give short tours, but people can also walk around on their own. We'll have drinks and food for everyone. And we'll hand out promotional pieces that give them a discount on a first booking."

"People won't come into our apartment, though, right?" I asked.

"That's correct," Dad said. "You don't ever have to worry about that. This apartment is our home and is completely separate from the inn."

"So Lindy and I can just stay up here and watch TV or whatever?" Davis asked before he shoved a big piece of meat into his mouth.

"Or do your homework," Dad replied.

Before Davis could object, Mom smiled and said, "School's out on Friday, remember?"

Dad sat back in his chair and smiled, too. "Ah, that's right." He took his glasses off and rubbed the bridge of his nose as he turned to Mom. "What are these kids going to do all summer long? You'll be busy with the inn and guests. Hopefully. I'm not taking time off from the firm until August."

"They're both signed up for some camps," Mom said. "We'll do some fun things around the city together when time permits. And beyond that, I'm counting on them to be resourceful and find things to occupy themselves."

"We do have friends, Dad," I said as I reached for another piece of bread. "Remember when you were a kid and spent the summer hanging out with friends? Or has your old brain forgotten what that was like?"

"Ouch," Dad said as he put his glasses back on. "And *you* know I'm not *that* old, right?"

I smiled. "I know. I was just joking."

"That reminds me," Mom said. "We probably need to have a discussion about whether we're ready for Lindy to ride the subway by herself. With most of her friends living in Brooklyn right now, I'm guessing she's going to be wanting to go there quite a bit."

Since we'd moved, Mom had hired a part-time nanny, an older, retired woman, to ride with Davis and me to and from school every day, since we still went to school in Brooklyn. I had told her we'd be fine by ourselves, but she'd said Dad didn't want us to do that yet.

"As I've said before, I feel pretty strongly that she should be thirteen," Dad said.

I'd turn thirteen on August 14. "But that's only a couple of months away."

"Yes," he said as he reached for more potatoes and carrots. "Which means we better get busy teaching you all the things you need to know in order to ride by yourself."

I looked at him, confused. "What kind of things?"

"Things that involve your safety," he replied. "What to do in different scenarios that might arise."

I resisted the urge to roll my eyes. "But I have a cell phone. And I know more than you probably think I do."

"Still, there is no such thing as being too safe," Dad said. "I think, for now, there'll be no riding without an adult. Julie, can you check and see if Frannie is available this summer to help with getting them to and from camps?"

Davis groaned. "Really? More time with Frannie the nanny? And just so you know, I don't think that's her real name. I think she made it up so it'd rhyme."

While they discussed whether someone would be silly enough to pick a name that rhymes with their job (Sawyer the lawyer, anyone?), I thought about what it all meant for me. I had imagined lots of freedom over the summer. Instead, I'd be tied to the B&B like a flag to a pole. But it'd be even worse because at least a flag gets to fly.

There once was a nanny named Frannie.
Nope.
Not doing it.
Not. Doing. It!!

Dear Parents
A poem by Lindy Mackay

You imagine monsters.
I imagine unicorns.
You imagine burnt toast.
I imagine blueberry muffins.
You imagine a thunderstorm.
I imagine a rainbow.
I think I feel sorry for you.

Chapter 5

NYPL: NEW YORK PUBLIC LIBRARY, AKA HEAVEN

Monday after school, Frannie watched from the sidewalk as I let Davis and myself into the inn. She had a key, too, but didn't need to come inside with us today. Outside of the library sat a big box of books. I got excited until I quickly thumbed through them and saw there weren't any specifically for kids.

"Someone's here," Davis said as he dropped his backpack on the shiny hardwood floor. There were voices coming from the dining room. "Come on. Let's go see who it is."

"There they are," Mom said when she saw us. "Vivian

was kind enough to drop off some books for our library. I was telling her you'd be home any minute. She wanted to say hello. Come and take a seat. I'll run upstairs and get you two a snack."

Vivian is a neighbor we met last year, when Mom and Dad first bought the B&B, before the renovations started. She lives in an apartment in the building next door and took the time to come over and say hello one day when Mom and Dad were meeting with the contractor. She even brought us homemade snickerdoodles. We all liked her right away, and not because of the cookies. Well, that's probably why Davis liked her. But she's one of those people who has a way of making you feel calm and relaxed, no matter what's going on, just by being around her.

She's an older woman with short brown hair who wears her reading glasses on a pretty beaded chain. My mother had commented on it the first time we met her and Vivian had told us, "Some of the beads are ocean jasper, which is believed to bring strength and renewal by eliminating stress. It is a stone of joy."

I'd thought to myself, *Maybe that's why she is the picture of calm.*

She went on to explain that since she's retired, she enjoys making jewelry during the winter, when she can't get outside as much. Being retired sounds so fun. You can just do whatever you want, whenever you want, and there's not a single school project to worry about.

Now Vivian sat at the end of one of the dining tables with a glass of iced tea in front of her. "How was school today?" she asked. "Learn anything exciting you'd care to share?"

"I learned that fractions are still not my friend," Davis said as he plopped into a chair next to Vivian.

"Ah, yes, the dreaded fractions," Vivian replied with a wink. "Don't fight them too hard and eventually they'll come around. You'll see. And what about you, Lindy?"

I set my messenger bag on the floor and pulled up a chair across from her. "I learned I am dreading our summer project more than ever. Our homeroom teacher gave us some time to brainstorm for the HAT project. You know, to make a plan or whatever. But I just feel lost."

"Forgive me if this should be obvious, but what's the HAT project?" she asked.

"HAT stands for Heart, Abilities, Talents. We're supposed to follow our heart to find our abilities and talents this summer to help us choose high schools to apply to next year."

She grinned. "Now, doesn't that sound interesting?"

I sighed. "Not if you don't even know where to start. Some people have it so easy. Like my friend Talia—she's always loved to dance." I turned to my brother. "And this guy here is probably going to be the next Babe Ruth."

Davis groaned. "Don't say that, Lindy. He was a Yankee."

"Okay, whatever, that's not my point. It's like you were born with a baseball mitt on your hand."

"I wish," Davis said. "Maybe the Mets would have recruited me right then!"

Vivian laughed before she turned to me. "You know, my grandson is coming to visit soon. He'll be here for a month or so, and I plan on taking him around the city. Would you like to join us? Maybe try some activities on for size and see what you think? I was a tour guide for many years and have lots of friends who would be glad to help, I'm sure."

I felt a wave of relief wash over me. This was exactly what I needed. "Really? That would be amazing!"

"What's amazing?" Mom said as she set bowls of sliced apples and pretzels in front of us.

"I've invited Lindy to go around the city with me and my grandson," Vivian replied. "If it's all right with you, of course. I have some fun things planned, and it would be nice to have someone about Tyler's age along with us to make it a bit more fun for him. And Lindy could work on her summer assignment."

"That is so nice of you to offer," Mom said. "Lindy and Davis have some camps they'll be going to, though. Would it be possible to work around those?"

"How about if we meet up on Saturdays?" Vivian asked.

"That would be perfect," Mom said.

"Wonderful," Vivian replied. She turned back to me. "Shall we plan on beginning the Saturday after the grand opening? We can adjust as we go along if we need to."

I nodded with a smile, but all of a sudden, I felt nervous. I didn't realize her grandson was my age. When she'd mentioned him earlier, I'd imagined him younger for some reason. Much younger. Would it be awkward hanging out with a boy? Some girls would probably be thrilled, but not me. The only boys I felt comfortable hanging out with were the ones I found in the pages of books.

I thought about "trying activities on for size," like Vivian had said, with a guy named Tyler standing by and watching me. This was not what I'd signed up for. Not only that, it sounded the exact opposite of amazing. No, it sounded like a big, awful pile of mud, and there I was, stuck right in the middle of it.

Mud

A poem by Lindy Mackay

I can't move.
Feet are stuck.
I'll wish for some sun
and a whole lot of luck.

Chapter 6

YANKEES OR METS: YOU CAN CHOOSE ONLY ONE

$\mathcal{E}$very day after school, Mom put me to work helping with stuff around the inn to get ready for the grand opening. On Tuesday, it was putting the books Vivian had given us into the bookshelf in the library. On Wednesday, it was cleaning the inside windows with Windex. On Thursday, it was dusting every square inch of the banister. This task did not make sense to me, the same way it wouldn't make sense if someone told me the weather forecast called for snow in June.

"Why do we need to do that?" I asked her.

"Well, because it gets dusty like every other surface in this old place."

"Will anyone even notice, though?"

"Yes. Someone will surely notice. I'm sorry, Lindy, I know it isn't the most fun thing in the world to be doing, but I bet you'll have it finished in no time. And once we have some guests and start bringing in some income, I'll hire a maid service. But for the time being, we have to do it ourselves."

I reluctantly got a dust rag and went down to the first floor.

When Dad came home a while later and saw me cleaning, he said, "Oh, good, your mom is making use of the free labor."

I stood up and stretched my hands up high over my head. "Dad, you're a lawyer. Aren't there laws against this kind of thing?"

He smiled. "It's completely acceptable to have you help out with the family business. Sorry, kiddo. Hey, is Davis around?"

"He went to Jacob's house after school," I said as I plopped down onto one of the steps. "They're going to bring him home after dinner."

"Perfect. I have a surprise for him, so I was hoping I'd have time to do something fun with it."

"A surprise?" I asked. "What is it?"

"Promise you won't tell?" he said as he set his briefcase down and pulled out a fancy gold envelope.

"I promise," I said.

"The firm has Mets season tickets behind home plate, and my name was drawn for two tickets to the Phillies game tomorrow night."

"But you have season tickets, too," I said.

"Yeah, but these are the best seats in the house." He picked up his briefcase and walked up the stairs. "Davis will be thrilled, trust me. Mom didn't want to go to the game tomorrow, since she has so much to do to get ready for Saturday. It's the perfect solution." All of a sudden, he looked concerned. "Are you okay with missing the game, Lindy?"

"Yeah," I said. "You know me. I mostly go for the concession stand."

"You're a good sport," he said with a smile as he walked by me. "I'm gonna go find your mom and tell her the good news. Thanks for your help, kiddo. You're doing a great job."

I sighed. "You're welcome."

It wasn't fair. I felt like Cinderella. Davis was out having fun with a friend, and when he came home, he'd have an amazing surprise waiting for him. Meanwhile, all I got was work, work, and more work.

I set my rag down and went to the front doors and peeked out one of the panel windows. It was such a nice day. Mom wouldn't mind if I stepped outside for a few minutes for some fresh air, would she?

No, I told myself. She wouldn't.

The stoop of our brownstone is one of my favorite things. It's big and wide, with black wrought-iron rails along both sides. Mom bought two huge clay pots and planted some bright pink geraniums to put next to the double front doors. Above the doors is a small sign that says *The Chorus Inn*.

I had yet to sit on the stoop, so that's what I did. I went down a few steps and took a seat. I didn't have my notebook with me or I might have pulled it out and written a few words. I thought about texting one of my friends, since I did have my phone with me, but it was kind of nice to sit there and do nothing for a change.

A tall boy with blond hair and wearing board shorts was walking a dog down the block. He stopped at the bottom of the stoop and said, "Hi."

"Hi. Pretty dog."

"Thanks."

"What's his name?"

"Odie."

"Odie?" I said. "Do you have a cat named Garfield, too?"

He smiled. "Nope. Just the dog. Hey, do you know if there's a pool close by?"

"I'm not really sure," I said. "We just moved in a few weeks ago."

His face changed. All of a sudden, it was like he recognized me, even though we had never met before. "Wait. Are you Lindy?"

"Yeah. How'd you know?"

"My grandma. She told me about you and your family."

I stood up. At the word *grandma*, something snapped inside of me, like a giant rubber band. This was Vivian's grandson. "You're Tyler?"

"Yep."

Relief washed over me. I'd been worried that he might be too cool for me. Or not very friendly. But he seemed nice. Plus, he had a dog.

I went down the steps. "That's great you got to bring Odie with you. Can I pet him?"

"Sure. He loves people."

"What kind is he?" I asked as I reached the bottom step.

"Golden retriever."

Odie's beautiful brown eyes stared into mine as I stroked his fur, and the longing for a dog that I kept pressed down all the time came rushing up. Ever since I went to Talia's tenth birthday party at her place and met her puppy, Rudy, a Scottish terrier, I've dreamed of having a dog—a small one who could sit on my lap while I read. If it were a boy, I'd name him Sparky. If it were a girl, I'd name her Honey. Obviously, I've thought about this a lot. If only my mom loved dogs as much as I do. One bit her on the hand when she was a kid, so she's scared of them now.

"I was hoping I could find a pool nearby," he said.

"The outdoor pools aren't open yet," I told him.

"Aw man," he said. "That is not what I wanted to hear."

"Sorry," I said. "When they do open, you could go with me and my brother. It's one of his favorite things to do in the summer, too."

His face lit up. "Really? That'd be awesome."

"And your grandma will do other fun things with you. I mean, it's New York City! There's a ton of stuff to do."

"Yeah, I know. I just love swimming. She told me you'll be going around the city with us on Saturdays. For a school project or something?"

"Right. She offered to help me with it." He didn't say anything. I couldn't tell if he was disappointed or what. "Hopefully it will be fun."

"Yeah," he said quietly, leaning down and petting Odie. "Hopefully."

Before I could say anything else, I heard the door open behind us, followed by Dad's voice. "Lindy, there you are. I came down to tell you dinner's almost ready, and you weren't there. Scared me for a second."

I turned around. "Sorry. Dad, this is Tyler, Vivian's grandson. And his dog, Odie."

Dad walked down, still wearing his dress shirt and slacks, and shook Tyler's hand. "Nice to meet you."

"You too," Tyler said. "I should go. I need to walk Odie around the block and get back for dinner. But I think we'll see you on Saturday."

"Oh, good, for the grand opening," Dad said. "See you then."

"Bye," I said.

Tyler gave us a wave before he took off with Odie down the sidewalk.

"So that's her grandson, huh?" Dad asked. "He seems nice."

"Yeah. He does." I couldn't help but wonder what Tyler thought about me, though.

"We should go up," Dad said as he took my hand. "Mom's gotta be wondering what happened to us. After dinner, you want to jam with your old man?"

"If it means I don't have to dust anymore, then yes," I said.

"You're getting better with the ukulele, you know," he said as we walked up the steps of our pretty porch, the bright pink flowers waving at us in the breeze.

"I don't think so," I replied.

"It's hard to see it when you're the one playing. Or doing anything, really. Try not to be so hard on yourself, huh?"

"I feel like that might be impossible."

He chuckled. "Well, maybe at twelve, it is. But hopefully not forever."

I sighed. "I think being twelve is just plain hard."

With a squeeze of my hand he said, "You may be right about that."

Random Thoughts

I've been thinking about Tyler and Odie a lot since I met them. I have questions. Many questions.

1. Why is he staying with his grandma for an entire month? That's a long time. Won't he get bored?

2. Where did he come from? That makes it sound like he's an alien. I mean, where does he live?

3. How old is he, exactly? She said he was about my age, but he might be a year older or a year younger or . . . who knows?

4. Does he like NYC?

5. Won't he miss his friends? And his family? Because a month is a really long time to be away from home. Oh yeah, I already said that.

I've never been away from home. The last two years, Mom tried to get me to agree to go summer camp and I said, "No way."

I don't want to go away to a place where I don't know anyone. Yes, I'd love to travel and see new places. Like, I would have loved going to Paris with Nora. But I don't want to go someplace new, by myself, and try to make friends.

"People do it all the time," Dad said when I was explaining my reasons. And I know it's true, but that doesn't mean I have to do it, does it? Making friends is hard. Especially when everyone is good at something. I'd just rather hang out with the friends I have or read books. There's nothing wrong with that. Is there?

Chapter 7

THE CITY: MANHATTAN

After school on our last day, there was a lot of screaming and yelling when the final bell rang. I'm not the screaming type, but I might have let out a small "Woo-hoo!" Maybe. Probably.

Because really, is there anything better than that feeling on the last day of school before summer vacation? I don't think so.

We'd cleaned out our lockers a couple of days before, so all I had was the backpack I'd carried with a notebook and a pencil inside. When I met up with Talia and Nora, like I always did after school, they were all smiles.

"We made it," Talia said, her graceful brown arms

reaching down to give me a hug. "We're top dogs now, can you believe it?"

"Please don't say that next year we'll *rule the school* like my dad did last night," Nora said. "We're eighth graders now, not royalty."

Talia and I laughed as we joined the stream of kids and headed toward the front doors. "Want to come over for a while?" Talia asked. "Mama said we could make some cookies-and-cream ice cream in our ice cream maker to celebrate. It's so good."

"Sure!" Nora said. "I can call my mom at work and let her know."

As soon as we stepped outside I eyed Frannie and Davis waiting for me in our normal meeting spot. "I can't," I said, gesturing toward them. "Sorry."

"Aw man," Talia said. "I'm sorry, too. I wish you still lived in Brooklyn."

At lunch a few days ago, I had told them what my dad had said about riding the subway by myself. Like good friends do, they'd let me whine and complain about it. Now there was really nothing to do but suck it up.

"Yeah," I said. "Me too. Have some ice cream for me."

"We will," Nora said as she gave me a quick hug bye. "See you tomorrow, though! I'm excited to see the place!"

"Okay, bye."

I watched for a moment as they scampered along

without me, taking all the school-is-out joy I'd felt just a couple of minutes ago right along with them.

"Come on, Lindy!" Davis yelled impatiently.

I glared at him.

"Everything all right?" Frannie asked me.

"Fine," I said. "Just wish I could go with my friends. They're so lucky they don't have to . . ." I almost said, "be followed around by a nanny." But that wouldn't have been very nice, even if it were true.

She nodded as we turned to go. "I understand. You're disappointed. Would it help you to know that when I was your age, I had to work in the summer, picking berries?"

Great. I was the one feeling left out and now she wanted me to feel sorry for *her*? "Nope. Doesn't really help," I muttered.

She continued talking. "I grew up in the state of Washington, and back then, kids could work in the berry fields. Things have changed now—stricter laws and all that. We didn't make much money, but our parents expected us to be out there earning something if we were able to. I made enough to buy myself a bicycle."

"Wow," Davis said. "I wish I could do that."

Frannie laughed. "It's hard work, though. Harder than you might think."

"How'd you get to the berry fields?" I asked.

"An old bus would drive around and pick us up," she said.

"Did a nanny have to go with you?" I asked. I knew I was being a brat, but sometimes when you're in a bad mood it's what comes naturally.

"I think you know the answer to that," she said. "We went alone. Or with our siblings, if we had them. It was a different time. Kids definitely had a lot more freedom. Anyway, my point in telling you all of that is you still have it pretty good. Yes, I'll have to take you into Brooklyn to see your friends. But you'll still get to go, right? If you were working the way I did when I was your age, you'd be missing out even more."

"I guess," I said.

I've always wondered why adults love playing the "it could be worse" game. It's like it's supposed to make us feel better, but it never really does because we still aren't getting what we want. I mean, why didn't she simply say, "It's okay. Be upset. You have every right to feel that way," and leave it at that?

"I also had to babysit my three younger siblings all the time," Frannie said as we made our way down the steps to the subway station. "You can probably imagine how fun that was."

"Do you feel lucky yet, Lindy?" Davis asked. "Aren't you glad you don't have to take care of me all day every

47

day? Hey, can we go out for doughnuts? That place in Chelsea Market is soooo good. Please, Frannie? To celebrate the last day of school?"

Frannie smiled. "Now, that is a fabulous idea. What do you say, Lindy? A doughnut will surely cheer you up, don't you think?"

One thing about Frannie, she loves sweets. Of course, doughnuts with my brother and my nanny wouldn't be nearly as fun as ice cream with my friends. Still, I was hungry. And those doughnuts were one of the best things we'd discovered since moving to Manhattan.

"Okay," I said.

"It's going to be all right," she said as we stood on the platform with all the other people, waiting for the train. "You'll see."

I could only respond with the same word Tyler had used with me on Thursday. "Hopefully."

The Monkey and the Rhino
A story by Lindy Mackay

Once there was a little monkey named Chunky who lived in a forest in Africa with lots of other monkeys. They were happy there, until humans came to plow down trees, and the monkeys had to find a new home.

The monkeys weren't able to stick together because there were too many of them. Finding a home big enough for all of them would have been too difficult. So they scattered across the jungle. Chunky's family ended up in trees on the edge of the forest. Sometimes when Chunky was high up in the tree, he would look down and see two rhinos, grazing in the grasslands nearby.

Chunky missed the other monkeys. He wanted to make new friends. So one evening he went into the grasslands to meet the rhinos. But when he talked to them, he realized they couldn't understand him because they didn't speak monkey.

How can I be friends with them if they don't speak my language? *Chunky thought. Not only that, he realized they didn't do the same things. Rhinos didn't climb trees. They didn't swing from branches. They didn't sit and groom their friends or family members. They seemed to do a lot of standing around. At least it seemed that way to little Chunky.*

Soon, the sun began to lower toward the earth, turning the sky bright orange and red. In the tall grass, Chunky had difficulty seeing the sun as it sank lower and lower. He wanted to watch until it disappeared completely.

He crept closer to the rhinos. And closer still. And when he was as near as he could be, he did the only thing left to do—he climbed up the back leg of one of the rhinos and found a comfortable spot in the middle of his back.

The monkey and the two rhinos watched the earth swallow the sun. It was like nothing he'd ever seen before—a spectacular show. He'd never watched the sunset because he'd been busy doing all the things that monkeys do.

He wanted to ask the rhinos, "Do you watch the sun set every evening?" But since they didn't speak the same language, he couldn't ask. All he could do was come back the next night to find out. What a nice surprise when he discovered them there again. And again. And again.

It wasn't long before Chunky spent every evening with the rhinos, watching the sunset. If the rhinos wandered away during the day, they made a point to come back to their special spot so Chunky could join them.

The rhinos could never be monkeys. And the monkey could never be a rhino. But they found a way to have fun together. Because that's what friends do. And that's what they were—friends.

Chapter 8

BODEGAS: CORNER STORES THAT SELL EVERYTHING

The big day arrived. Mom and I got up early Saturday morning, but Dad and Davis slept in since they'd been out late at the game the night before. Around eleven, all four of us walked to the bodega with the best flowers and brought home a bunch of different bouquets. Mom said fresh flowers are one of the best things you can do to make a place feel warm and welcoming.

Mom and I went to work putting the flowers into vases at the dining room table while Dad and Davis prepared trays of snacks for our guests. We were serving cheese and crackers, veggies and hummus, and some adorable sugar cookies in the shape of a brownstone.

"This is fun," I told Mom as I stuck a sunflower into a vase with a pink rose.

Mom shook her head and took the rose out of the vase. "Those don't really go together, Lindy. Why don't you use the white daisies with the sunflowers? I'm going to do some simple bouquets with just roses in these square vases. See?" She cut a few roses down fairly short and stuck them in the vase to show me. "Isn't that pretty?"

"Sorry," I muttered. "I've never done this before."

"Oh, sweetie, did I hurt your feelings? I didn't mean to. It's just that some colors go together more than others, you know? And the texture and style of the flower matters, too. It takes a bit of practice, I suppose. I've been looking at a lot of bouquets online, so I have some ideas in mind. I should have told you that before we started."

"It's okay," I replied. "At least this is more fun than dusting."

"Next time I'll let you pick out some flowers and make a bouquet any way you'd like. How's that?"

"I'm just not sure I'm very artistic," I said. "You've seen the paintings and drawings I've brought home from school. I'm really not good at that kind of thing. Like, to me, all colors go together. Why wouldn't they? They're colors!"

Mom laughed. "Well, when you say it that way, I see your point. Just so you know, I love your artwork. Art is what you make of it. There's really no right or wrong way."

"But some people are *so* good at it," I said as I stuck a few daisies into the vase with a couple of small sunflowers.

"And some people also practice a lot."

"I guess. I think there's more to it, though. I feel like some people are born with a special talent. Or maybe everyone is, but only some actually figure out what it is."

Just then, Dad and Davis walked in. "What's for lunch?" Davis asked. "I'm starving."

Mom glanced at the big decorative clock on the wall. It was almost twelve thirty. "Oh my gosh, lunch! I almost forgot."

"Why don't you keep working, and I'll make us some sandwiches?" Dad said.

"Thanks, honey," Mom said. "That's a big help. Though don't make anything for me. I'm too nervous to eat anything right now."

Dad gave her a disapproving look. "Julie, it's going to be fine. You'll see."

"I hope so."

"I know so," Dad said.

We finished with the flowers and put the vases in various places on the first floor. The vase I'd worked on, with the sunflowers and daisies, went next to the sign-in sheet, where people could sign up for the newsletter Mom planned on emailing out every once in a while.

After Dad, Davis, and I scarfed down some tuna fish sandwiches upstairs, Dad said he was going to join Mom and wait for the guests to show up.

"When Nora gets here, send her up, okay?" I told him.

"You sure you don't want to come down and help greet people?" he asked.

"Absolutely positive."

"Okay. If you say so."

After he left, Davis asked me, "Want to play Mario Kart?"

"No, thanks. I'm just gonna hang out in my room and read or something until Nora gets here."

"Aw man, you're no fun," Davis said.

"Oh, look at that, a late-breaking story—little brother thinks older sister is boring. More news at eleven," I said as I walked toward the bathroom.

"You're weird," he called out to me.

"And you smell like tuna fish," I said. "Brush your teeth after I'm done brushing mine."

"You're not my mother!"

And he couldn't understand why I'd rather hang out in my room alone?

Brothers
A poem by Lindy Mackay

Poppies are red,
the sky is blue,
tuna fish stinks,
and brothers do, too.

Chapter 9

THE VILLAGE: GREENWICH VILLAGE, OR THE WEST VILLAGE;

A HISTORIC NEIGHBORHOOD IN MANHATTAN

indy, somebody's here to see you!" Davis yelled a little while later.

I hadn't heard anyone knock. I threw my books onto my bed and rushed out of my room. "Nora, I'm so happy—"

But then I stopped when I turned the corner, because it wasn't Nora. It was Tyler.

"Oh, hi," I somehow managed to say. "I thought you were—"

"Nora," he said with a smile as he brushed the blond

bangs out of his eyes. "Yeah. I can see that. Sorry. Do you want me to go?"

My brother was sitting on the sofa with the controller in his hand and a big sheepish grin on his face. I shook my head. "Oh, no, it's fine. Do you want . . ."

I started to invite him into my room, but I hardly knew him, so it seemed strange to do that.

"Do you want something to drink? I think we have lemonade."

"Sure."

He followed me to the kitchen. "My grandma will be here in a few minutes. Your parents said it was all right if I came up to say hi. It's really cool you guys have an apartment up here and your guests stay in the rooms downstairs. Will you have to help make breakfast? You know, since it's a bed-and-breakfast?"

I went to the fridge as Tyler took a seat at the kitchen table. "I hope not. Helping to keep the place clean is bad enough. And I'm pretty sure no one wants to eat the toast I burn every time I make it. Besides, I think my mom said something about keeping it simple with oatmeal, fruit, yogurt, and pastries. New York City is full of great bakeries. Might as well let them do the work, right?"

I filled two glasses with lemonade and took them to the table. It seemed like this was my chance to ask him some of the questions I had, but I didn't want him to think I was nosy. Even though that's pretty much what I was. I couldn't help it, though. And besides, wasn't it fair that I know as much about him as he knew about me?

"So where do you live normally? I mean, when you're not staying with your grandma?" I asked as I tucked my hair behind my ears.

He took a drink of his lemonade before he answered. "Lakewood, Ohio. Outside of Cleveland."

"Oh," I said. "So that's not *too* far. Did you drive here, then? Oh, wait, I guess you must have, with Odie."

"Yeah, my dad drove us here. And I know you're probably wondering why I'm staying so long, so I'll just tell you." He spun his glass around and around on the table. I took a sip of my drink, suddenly feeling kind of nervous. "My parents are having some problems," he said as he looked up at me. "They're trying to work things out, and they thought it might be good if I came here while they do that. I guess they didn't really want me in the way or whatever?"

It came out as a question, and kind of made me feel uncomfortable. How can a kid possibly be in the way of his parents? They're a family.

"I'm sorry," I said. "Maybe they thought coming here would be more fun than being there. It's your summer vacation, you know? Like, that's supposed to be fun."

"I know. But I miss my friends. And our neighborhood pool. We go swimming almost every day in the summer. I love it. When I get to high school, I plan on trying out for the swim team."

Of course he missed his friends, the same way I'd miss mine if I went away for a month. I couldn't help but feel bad for him. We'd definitely have to take him swimming.

"So I guess swimming's your thing, then?"

He looked confused. "My thing?"

"Yeah. That thing you love to do and that you're good at."

"Oh, I see. I guess you could say that. One of them, anyway."

Great. He had more than one thing? I didn't even want to know what the others were. All I needed was to feel even more like I was already failing the HAT assignment.

"What do you like to do?" he asked. He seemed genuinely curious, and his green eyes were kind. Still, it was hard to talk about my problem to someone I hadn't known very long. Before I could answer, there was a knock at the front door.

"I'll get it!" Davis called out.

Saved by the bell. Or the knock. Whatever. "Maybe Nora's here," I said, glad for the interruption.

"Or my grandma. But before I go, I want to guess what it is you do."

"Oh no," I said. "Please don't." Because no matter what he'd say, I'd have to tell him he was wrong. Not only that, he might hurt my feelings in the process because what if he made the horrible assumptions most people did that had to do with the fact that I'm Asian? Like, why do so many people think I must be good at math and music? Stupid stereotypes.

I stood up just as Vivian walked into the kitchen.

"What are you trying to guess?" she asked him. Then she smiled at me and said, "Hello, Lindy."

"Hi."

Now Tyler stood up. "We were talking about swimming, and I wanted to know what she likes to do. That's all."

Vivian swooped in to save me, thank goodness. "Actually, that's what we are going to try to discover this summer, together. I didn't go into a lot of detail when I was telling you about Lindy's school project. But I'll fill in the blanks for you on our way home. It's going to be fabulous."

She sounded so certain. Why couldn't I feel that confident?

When there was another knock at the door, Davis

yelled, "Your turn to get it, Lindy, since they're all here to see you anyway!"

It made Vivian laugh. "We better get out of your hair."

I walked them to the door and opened it. Nora seemed surprised to see more than just me standing there.

"Vivian and Tyler, this is my friend Nora."

"Hi," Tyler said.

"So nice to meet you," Vivian said. "We're just leaving. You girls have fun."

"We will. Thanks for coming by," I said.

"See you later, Lindy," Tyler said as he slipped past me, behind his grandma.

Nora raised her eyebrows as if to say, "What is going on and why did you have a cute boy in your apartment?"

I waited until I closed the door to let my giggle escape.

"Who was that?" Nora asked.

"Our neighbors," I said as Davis yelled, "Her boyfriend!"

I glared at him. "He is not. I don't want a boyfriend, tuna breath, so be quiet."

Nora looked around our apartment. "This is really nice, Lindy."

"Thanks. Come on. The butterflies are waiting to say hello."

When she stepped into my room, her eyes scanned the four butter-yellow walls, one of them tastefully covered with painted butterflies, along with my bookshelf and the adorable window seat, and said, "Oh my gosh. Can I move in here with you?"

That is probably one of the best compliments your best friend can give you.

Here's What Happened the Past Twenty-Four Hours

3:30 p.m. *Nora left our place with her mom because they needed to go shopping for some new sandals. I was jealous. I want new sandals.*

    4:00 p.m. *Davis complained that he was hungry. I told him to go find the cookies shaped like brownstones and sneak a couple for us. He came back a few minutes later with four cookies along with some cheese and crackers wadded up in a napkin. It kind of felt like we were prisoners in a castle and he'd snuck away to the kitchen and smuggled food out when no one was looking.*

    4:19 p.m. *Those cookies were soooooooo good!*

    5:07 p.m. *Mom and Dad returned to the apartment and said the grand opening had been a huge success. Normally, we order Chinese food on Saturday nights, but Dad suggested we go out to eat for a change. Davis and I played rock, paper, scissors to decide who would get to pick the restaurant. After Davis won and chose Olive Garden, Mom, Dad, and I looked at each other and kind of rolled our eyes. When I said, "Really?" he argued his case for the all-you-can-eat breadsticks for like five minutes. I bet he'll grow up to be a lawyer like Dad.*

6:00 p.m. *Dinner at Olive Garden in Times Square. So many better places we could have gone to, but when Mom let me get chocolate cake for dessert, I was no longer unhappy about Davis choosing the restaurant.*

9:00 p.m. *Back home I got into bed, and read a Kate DiCamillo book for two hours. I love her books so much.* Because of Winn-Dixie *is another reason I wish I could have a dog.*

8:48 a.m. *Woke up and read some more until I smelled bacon cooking. Ate breakfast with the family, then took a shower, and this is where it gets really exciting!*

11:05 a.m. *Mom got a call on her cell phone. When she was finished, she told me to go downstairs because Vivian wanted to see me. So I ran downstairs to see her. She was there with Odie and Tyler. I petted Odie, who wagged his tail like he was really happy to see me. I said hello to Tyler. And THEN the most amazing thing happened. Vivian handed me a little velvet box and told me to open it. Inside was a necklace with a key on it! She said, "I want you to keep the faith because you will find your special talent. Right now it's just hidden and locked away somewhere, waiting patiently for you to find and open it. Every place we visit will open a new door for you."*

I was shocked. I told her thank you, but it didn't seem like enough. The necklace is so cute! I put it on right away, and it felt like it was made for me.

64

11:15 a.m. *Vivian said she and Tyler were on their way to the bakery around the corner to get some goodies and asked me if I wanted to come along. So not only did I get a new necklace, I also got a doughnut.*

It was a very good day.

Chapter 10

BRIDGE-AND-TUNNEL: LIVING OUTSIDE MANHATTAN, I.E., NEEDING A BRIDGE OR A TUNNEL TO GET TO "THE CITY"

Mom hadn't scheduled any camps for Davis or me during the first week of summer vacation, which meant we could sleep in. Except as much as I love the idea of sleeping in, I'm not always able to actually do it. I try, believe me. I wake up and lie there, hoping I'll be able to go back to sleep, but I never do. So I usually end up grabbing my book from the nightstand and reading in bed for a little while, letting my family *think* I'm still asleep. It feels a little bit sneaky even though I'm not doing anything wrong. Or maybe I *am* doing something wrong because if

I got up and went into the kitchen, Mom might say something like, "Oh good, you're up, you can help me with . . ."

So it was a rainy gray Tuesday morning and as I pretended to sleep but read my book instead, I heard my parents' voices. Neither of my parents are very loud people so it was strange that I could hear them. As I listened, I realized it was because they were arguing.

"We have to get some business soon," Dad said. "The bills are piling up, and without any income coming in—"

"Kevin, don't you think I know that?" Mom said. She said it with a tone I hardly ever heard her use. "I'm doing everything I can to get the word out. It's just going to take some time. Please don't put additional pressure on me. I'm stressed enough as it is."

"I'm sorry you're stressed. But I am, too. I didn't realize how difficult it would be to get people interested in staying here. Are we charging too much?"

"I don't think so. We're new, that's all. And please remember, we do have some reservations later this summer. Until then, without any online reviews for a while, it's going to be difficult. I've heard there are places where we could buy reviews, if you want to consider—"

"Julie, are you kidding me? We are not going to stoop to something so low. What if someone found out we'd done that? It'd be the end of everything we've worked so hard for. No, we have to wait and get some good reviews the old-fashioned way—because people *want* to give them to us."

The way he said it made me sit straight up in bed. He sounded *really* angry. And it made me upset for my mother. She hadn't done anything wrong. She was trying to come up with some ideas, that's all. How could he be mad at her for that?

I didn't want to hear any more. And so I got up and opened my bedroom door. "Hey, Mom? I'm awake. Should I get some cereal for breakfast, or are you going to make something?"

"Pancakes!" Davis yelled from his room. "I want pancakes. Please? Pretty, pretty please, sweet mother of ours? One shaped like a rabbit and the other in the shape of a snake."

Good old Prince Charming, turning on the charm again. One of our mother's special talents is making pancakes in simple animal shapes. At some point, Davis will be like me and won't care what shape his pancakes come in, but clearly that day wasn't today.

Knowing Davis was awake made me wonder if he had heard our parents arguing, too. Did it worry him like it worried me? My mind instantly went to Tyler. My parents got along really well. Like, they hardly ever fought. So what did it mean, them suddenly arguing like this?

Nothing, I told myself. *It's one disagreement, that's all.* Tyler would probably tell me his parents had been arguing for years. Although he'd only tell me that if I decided to ask him about it, which would be awkward for both of us. I wasn't even sure how a conversation like that would go.

Hey, so, I'm curious, but what did you mean, exactly, when you said your parents are having problems?

Davis asked me once what *cringe-worthy* means— perfect example, right there.

"Okay," Mom called out. "I'll make pancakes. But you kids have to help. Meet me in the kitchen in five."

Saved by pancakes. Thank goodness. I jumped out of bed and threw on some shorts and a hoodie. Then I went into the kitchen. Davis was there; Mom wasn't. I waited to see if Davis would mention the arguing, but he didn't say a word. Part of me wanted to say something, to talk about it with someone, but the other part of me knew it was probably best to keep it to myself. Besides, he probably would have told me it didn't mean anything and that I was being dramatic. And maybe I was. All I knew was that I didn't want it to happen again.

"It's raining," Davis groaned. "I wonder what we're gonna do today."

"I don't know, but please don't demand Mom take us somewhere. She has a lot going on. The last thing we should be doing is stressing her out."

"Maybe it'll stop raining and be sunny later. We should ask if she'll take us to the pool."

"Davis, did you hear what I just said? Besides, the pools aren't even open, remember?"

"Aw man, that's no fair."

When Mom appeared a minute later, she looked kind of like a lost little child in her fuzzy pink bathrobe and her wavy blond hair all flat on one side. I had a sudden urge to give her a hug. So that's what I did.

"Is everything all right, Lindy?" she asked as she wrapped her arms around me.

"I love you. That's all."

I felt her relax into the hug. "Aw. That's nice. Thank you. I love you, too." She kissed the top of my head before she said, "Now, let's get those pancakes made, what do you say?"

I went to the cupboard and grabbed the mixing bowl as Mom started getting out the ingredients.

"What are we going to do today?" Davis asked. I turned around and glared at him. He shrugged and looked at me like, "What?"

Mom sighed. "I don't know. I need to work on the inn's website; I have some ideas I want to implement. Should I call Frannie? See if she can take you kids somewhere?"

Before either of us could respond, Dad appeared, dressed and ready for work. I watched him closely, curious if he'd say anything to Mom about their conversation earlier. It seemed to me like he should apologize, but maybe he wouldn't want to do that in front of Davis and me.

"You want to stay for some breakfast?" Mom asked him. "It won't be too long before it's ready."

"No, thanks. I need to get going. I'll pick up something at the coffee shop."

Was that a hint of disappointment on Mom's face? I couldn't tell for sure.

Dad went over to Mom and kissed her on the cheek. "Have a good day."

He turned and tousled Davis's hair. "You too." He looked over at me. "Be good to each other, all right?"

"Bye, Dad," Davis said.

I chimed in also. "See ya later."

After he left, Mom picked up her phone. "I'm going to call Frannie. I hadn't scheduled her for today, but if she's free, that'll be for the best, I think."

I started to protest and then decided not to. The

B&B needed guests. Maybe the best thing we could do was leave Mom alone so she could work.

"I wish there was something we could do to help," I told Mom as I went to the cupboard to get some plates.

This time, Mom let out an even louder sigh. "Me too, Lindy. Me too."

The Lonely Princess—Part 1
A story by Lindy Mackay

Once, there was a princess, named Li, who lived in a palace in China. Her life as a princess was very boring. Every day after she woke up, a servant would bring her rice porridge for breakfast along with some tea. After breakfast, the servant would help Li get dressed into one of the many silk dresses she owned. Once dressed, Li took a walk outside in the garden if it was a nice day. If she couldn't go outside, she would stay in her room, reading. Eventually a tutor would arrive and give her lessons in different subjects. Later in the day, she would join her mother and father, the emperor and empress, for a meal, where they hardly talked at all.

With no brothers or sisters, and no friends to play with, Li was sad and lonely. One day, instead of walking in the garden or reading, she walked from room to room in the palace and counted. After she'd walked down every hallway and been from one corner of the palace to the other, she gasped at what she now knew. The palace had two hundred and eighteen rooms. And for what? The staff stayed in some of them, but they didn't need even half that many.

This new knowledge gave Li an idea. "Why don't we allow people to come and visit the palace, and stay in the rooms that go unused?" she asked her father as they ate their evening meal of soup, rice, and fish.

The emperor frowned. "Why would we want to do that? Besides, I have no time for such small matters. I'm busy with my duties."

"Then let me do it," Li said. "I will put up notices around town. Please, Father? Please, won't you consider it?"

"I have just one question," her mother said softly. "Why do you want to do this? Allow strangers into your home?"

Li put her chopsticks down and said, "Mother, it is not a home. It is a palace. A lonely palace for a young girl like me. If we let people come and stay here, I will have people to talk to and things to do. We could also ask people to pay a fee, and use the money to help the poor."

Li's mother looked at her father. "It sounds like a lovely idea to me. What do you think?"

"My daughter, if you can get people here, to this lonely palace, as you call it, then I will allow it. But it may not be as simple as you think it may be."

"What do you think it will take to get people to stay here?" Li's mother asked her.

Li began eating her soup again. "I don't think I know just yet. But I will figure it out. In time, I will have the perfect solution."

Chapter 11

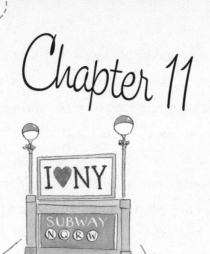

UPTOWN: NORTH, BASICALLY

Frannie was free that afternoon so she took us to the Museum of Natural History. The dinosaur exhibit has always been Davis's favorite. We hadn't been there in a few years, and I thought maybe he would have grown out of his obsession but no such luck. I've never understood the fascination. They're just a bunch of old bones from humongous creatures that lived millions of years ago. Personally, I find a living, breathing dog that you can pet, snuggle, and play games with much more interesting.

On Wednesday, even though Mom said she'd spend the day with us, she ended up calling Frannie again and having her take us to see a matinee showing of *Matilda* on Broadway. We all loved it, but it would have been more fun if Mom had gone along with us.

Every day she seemed more and more stressed, and that stressed *me* out. On Thursday, she apologized again, telling us she needed to keep working. "I've got to try to get more exposure somehow," she told us. "It really seems like the only solution to me. In order for people to want to stay here, they have to know we exist first. It's as simple as that."

I don't know why, but it didn't seem as simple as that to me. I didn't say anything, though, because I couldn't think of any other suggestions to give her.

"What will do today?" Davis asked Thursday morning as we all sat at the kitchen table, eating toast. Though Mom wasn't eating anything, just sipping on her coffee. The bags under her eyes seemed darker. Had she and Dad been arguing again? Was she having trouble sleeping? I could have asked, but I didn't because she probably would have told me not to worry, that everything was fine. That's what good parents do—they try their best to keep their kids from worrying.

"Well," Mom said, "what do you think about going to Brooklyn this afternoon to see your friends? Is there somewhere you could all meet up? Or should I call and see if Nora's and Jacob's parents would have you over for the afternoon? I'm thinking Frannie could drop you off, run some errands for me, and then pick you up a few hours later and bring you home?"

"Yeah!" Davis said with a fist pump. "Let's do that."

Mom looked at me. "What do you think, Lindy?"

"Isn't that sort of rude? Inviting ourselves over like that?"

"You're not inviting yourselves over," she said as she got up and took her cup to the sink. "I'm asking if it'd be all right if you came over to play for a while. Well, you and Nora don't really play anymore, but you know what I mean. They'll know they'd be doing me a favor, and of course I'm happy to return it someday."

I shrugged. "Okay. I mean, I'd love to see Nora."

"Great. Let me make those calls."

That afternoon, Nora and I sat on her bedroom floor as we flipped through magazines and painted each other's nails. I'd painted hers light blue, and now she was painting mine lavender. I'd told her about my parents' argument, curious to find out what she thought about it all.

"No one gets along all the time, right?" she said as she dipped the brush into the polish before running it across my pointer finger. "Except maybe us." She looked up at me and grinned.

"We got in a fight once," I replied. "Remember? In fourth grade. You thought we should wear matching costumes because we both wanted to be Hermione for Halloween. But I didn't want to do that, so then I had to come up with something else."

"Okay, well, there you go," Nora said as she went back to focusing on my nails. "No one gets along all the time. I still think we could have both been Hermione and it would have been fine. But your Pippi Longstocking was *ah*-mazing. It all worked out, right?"

"Yeah, thanks to my mom, who got the wig and the striped tights and everything." I paused. "I'm curious. Do you think your parents argue very much?"

She dipped the brush again. "Hm. I've never really thought about it. I guess they don't. My grandpa, my mom's dad, annoys my dad sometimes. And my mom doesn't like it when Dad complains about him. So they do argue about that once in a while." She finished up and put the brush back in the jar. "Why are you so worried about this anyway?"

I blew on my fingers before I answered. "I don't know. Maybe it's because Tyler is here visiting his grandma so his parents can have some time alone to work out their problems. It's like he's made me paranoid or something."

"So tell me more about what you guys are doing together this Saturday," Nora said. "Your texts didn't explain it very well. Maybe you should have used more emojis to make your point."

It made me laugh. "But I used the key emoji, which is the perfect one to go along with what we're doing." I pulled the necklace out from underneath my T-shirt, careful not to smudge my nails. "See what Vivian gave me? Isn't it the cutest?"

She leaned in and looked at it. "Oh my gosh, I love it."

"I don't know much about the plan, really," I explained. "Just that Vivian wants to help unlock my special talent. So we're going to go around the city, visit places, and try things out, I guess? She used to be a tour guide and knows lots of people. I just hope I don't embarrass myself. I mean, Tyler's all right, but still, this could turn out to be a disaster."

"Or it could turn into your first true love," Nora said as she wiggled her eyebrows at me.

"Ha-ha, very funny. Like I need another thing in my life to worry about. We're just friends, and it's gonna stay that way."

"Okay, okay." She studied her pretty blue nails. "Maybe your special talent is nail painting. You did a really good job on mine. Better than I did on yours."

I sat up straight and tall. "I did do a good job, didn't I? Except, I don't really *love* painting nails the way you love Paris. By the way, what's happening with the cello?"

"Oh, I should have showed it to you! It's downstairs. Mom let me rent one for the summer. I start lessons tomorrow."

I wiggled my fingers. "Now your nails will sparkle as you play."

"Right? Want to paint each other's toes next?"

"Um, only if we paint our own."

Nora tried to look shocked. "You mean you don't want to touch my toes? What kind of best friend are you?"

"The kind who loves hanging out with you but would rather kiss a snake than touch someone else's toes."

She laughed. "Kiss a snake? Ewww. Where do you come up with these things, Lindy? Comedy club, I'm telling you."

Pedicure, Please!

A limerick by Lindy Mackay

There once was a toe that looked funny
and wished to hide when the weather was sunny.
But it's hard to do that,
like bad hair in a hat,
so to polish it said, "Come here, honey!"

Chapter 12

DOWNTOWN: SOUTH, BASICALLY

When Saturday rolled around, I was glad the sun had replaced the rain we'd had on and off all week. After I woke up and checked my phone for messages and the weather, I got out of bed and headed straight for the shower.

"Good morning, sunshine," Dad said, coming out of his room just as I came out of mine. He was dressed like he might be going into the office.

"Are you going to work today?"

"Yeah. Stuff is piling up. I can't get too far behind or I won't be able to take my vacation later this summer.

You know I have to work on the weekends sometimes. That's just how it goes."

"But . . ."

He looked at me with concern. "What is it?"

The truth was I didn't want him to go. I wanted him to stay home and help Mom with stuff. And when I got home later, I wanted all of us to be together, to have our usual Saturday-night dinner of Chinese food and maybe watch a movie afterward. I wanted to know, for sure, that everything was fine.

"Is Mom okay with it?" I asked.

He gave me a funny look. "Sure. Why wouldn't she be? I should be back in time to take Davis to his game late this afternoon. And tomorrow the four of us will go to the Mets game. Should be a great day for it. See? You'll get plenty of time with me this weekend. Besides, this afternoon you'll be out and about with Vivian and Tyler. You won't even miss me." He tousled my hair like he loved to do. "I better run. Be good. And remember, be aware of your surroundings at all times, okay?"

"Safety first. I know, Dad. I'll be fine."

"See ya later."

"Bye."

After he left, I walked down the narrow hallway to their bedroom and peeked my head in. Mom sat at the small white desk in the corner as she looked at something on her laptop. Since there isn't room for an office in our apartment, she either works at the desk in her room or at the kitchen table.

"Mom?" I said softly so I wouldn't startle her.

She turned around. She was sitting there in her robe and slippers. "Hi, honey. Come on in. You're up bright and early for a Saturday. Excited about spending the afternoon with Vivian and Tyler?"

Excited wasn't the word I would use, but I didn't say that. "I guess so. I was just wondering, well, I saw Dad leave. Is everything all right?"

"Of course. He needs to get some work done at the office."

"You don't need his help with anything?" I asked as I leaned against the door, fiddling with the doorknob, keeping my eyes down.

"Like what?"

I shrugged. "I don't know. Couldn't he help with the B&B stuff? This place belongs to him, too, right?"

"Yes, but he has a regular job, and this is supposed to be my job. So for the most part, I need to handle the inn stuff myself." I looked up at her and saw that she now had a concerned look on her face. "Honey, is something bothering you?"

I shook my head. "No. I just wanted to check on you, that's all."

"I'm sorry if my worries have got *you* worried. I need to be more careful about what I say around you kids. Everything is going to be fine. Believe me?"

I nodded. Even though that was exactly what I'd expected her to say and I wasn't a hundred percent sure that I really did believe it.

A little before one o'clock, I said good-bye to Mom and Davis and went down the stairs slowly, counting as I went. I was thankful to Vivian for offering to help me, but I was nervous. Really nervous.

Outside, it was warm. I looked up and couldn't help but smile at the bright blue sky with big, fluffy clouds rolling by. It really felt like summer now. After lunch, I'd gone to my room to get ready, and I'd changed my clothes three times as I tried to figure out what to wear. At first, I thought I should dress to impress, as my dad likes to say, so I'd put on my favorite green dress. But it seemed way too fancy. Next I put on a skirt and blouse, and that didn't feel right, either. I'd thought about wearing my black pants, but that seemed kind of boring. So I'd ended up in my favorite pair of jeans with low-wedge sandals and a T-shirt that said *Keep calm and eat doughnuts.* I fingered my key necklace, hoping we'd have a good day and I'd find something that I seriously *loved* to do.

When I saw Vivian and Tyler walking toward me, I waved.

"Hello, Miss Lindy," Vivian said with a smile when they reached me.

"Hello," I said. Feeling a little shy, I found myself wishing Odie were there. "Odie had to stay home?"

Tyler replied, "Yeah. He wanted to come with us, but Grandma said he'd be better off at home. He's well trained, but it's no fun being tied up outside while we're going somewhere he can't go."

"Yeah. That makes sense." I turned to Vivian. "Do you know what we're doing first?"

"I do. But I think I'll wait and let it be a surprise."

"Do we have to take the subway?"

"Nope. We're going to stay in the Village this afternoon. I figure next Saturday we can wander a little farther. But there are plenty of things to see right here in our own little corner of the city."

We walked quietly for a couple of blocks, and then Vivian asked what my brother and I had been up to the last week. When I told them we'd seen the play *Matilda*, she said, "Oh, I wonder if Tyler would like that. Maybe I should take him."

"It's pretty funny," I told them. "A few of the songs were kind of boring, though. Do you like musicals?" I asked Tyler.

"Sort of?" Tyler said with a big grin, showing off his straight white teeth. "Every time I come and visit Grandma, she takes me to one. We've seen *The Lion King*, *Annie*, *Seussical*, and a couple of others I can't remember. *Lion King* was my favorite."

"Yeah, I loved that one, too."

"All right, dears," Vivian said as she stopped in front of us. "We're here."

I stopped and looked up, taking in what "here" meant. And I could hardly believe what I saw.

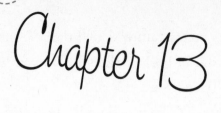

Chapter 13

HOUSTON: THE STREET THAT MARKS THE BEGINNING OF DOWNTOWN NEIGHBORHOODS LIKE SOHO (SOUTH OF HOUSTON); PRONOUNCED "HOW-STON"

But everyone loves this," I said to Vivian. "Don't they?"

"Except for people who are lactose intolerant," Tyler joked.

"You may love eating it, Lindy, but do you love *making* it?" Vivian asked as she gave me a little wink. "That's what we're going to try to discover today."

"I'm going to make pizza?" I asked her.

"This was one of the favorite stops when I gave tours around the West Village. People absolutely adore Joe's Pizza. You've never eaten here before?" .

"No. Not yet." I peered through the front window. The place wasn't very big, and there were quite a few customers waiting to get food. "Are you sure it's okay if I do this?"

"It's a bit out of the ordinary, I know, but the manager said it's fine. They'll help you make a pizza, and then we'll eat it."

This made Tyler extremely happy. "So this is why we only had salads for lunch. Awesome. I can't wait."

"Is Tyler going to help me?" I asked, not quite sure if I wanted her to answer yes or no. Davis and I helped out Mom and Dad in the kitchen sometimes, but I didn't do much in the way of cooking by myself. To me, it seemed like a lot of work when I could just as easily have a bowl of cereal or a peanut butter sandwich.

"There's only enough room for you back there, but we'll be nearby," Vivian said. I glanced at Tyler, and it seemed to me that he looked a little disappointed by that response. She gave my shoulder a little squeeze. "You're going to be fine. You'll see!"

We made our way inside and got in line. Vivian stood on her tippy toes and waved at one of the guys behind the counter. He motioned for us to come forward, so we went around the customers and up to the counter.

"You must be Lindy," the short man with a mustache said, his elbows crossed in front of him on the counter. "Great to meet you. Now, I have just one question for you."

I gulped. Was he going to ask if I knew how to make pizza? Or maybe he wanted to know if I had a license of some kind to cook in a restaurant? Or what if he wanted to know whether or not I'd ever eaten there before? I bit my lip as I waited for the question, sure that I would humiliate Vivian and myself with the answer.

He stood up tall, held his hands in the air, and said, "Are you-a ready to make-a the best-a pizza pie-a in the whole-a city of New York?"

I couldn't decide if he was trying to be funny or if that was simply his lame attempt at sounding Italian, so I just sort of smiled at him. You'd think people would have given him strange looks, but that's New York for you. It didn't faze a single person. They just kept on talking.

As for me, I was equal parts excited and terrified and couldn't help but wonder if maybe this was a really bad idea. What if I messed up? What if I chopped off my finger or even worse, burnt the thing and caught the place on fire? I mean, I could barely make toast.

He smiled at me. "Well?"

"I think so?" I replied.

Then he laughed. "Don't be nervous. This is going to be fun, you'll see. Come back here and put on your apron."

He lifted the top of the hinged counter so I could

step through to the kitchen behind him. There were two men working back there, one of them slicing up a big cheese pizza and the other one checking the pizzas that were in the oven.

"I'm Harold, by the way," the man with the mustache said. "I'm going to help you make the pizza." He pointed to the guys in the kitchen. "That's Mike and Steve. And the guy at the register ringing up orders is Rocco." He took an apron from a hook. "Want to put your bag here?" I did as he said before I took the apron from him. "Put that on and then wash your hands in the sink over there."

When I was finished, I went and stood next to Harold at the counter.

"You ever tossed a pie before?"

I shook my head hard, hoping that would be enough to convince him that asking me to do that might be a mistake. But he just smiled and said, "Well, there's a first time for everything, right?"

There were two round wedges of dough, each the size of a small plate, sitting in front of us.

"First," Harold explained, "we need to cover them in flour, like this." He placed one of the wedges in a big, round metal bowl of flour and turned it over, covering it well on both sides. He took it out and tossed it on the counter. "Now do yours."

When my dough was floured like his, he said, "Next,

we're going to press it out with our fingers. But stay away from the outer edge. That's the crust." We both worked our fingers in and around the dough for a long time, and slowly, the wedges were becoming flatter. I followed his lead when he flipped the dough over and flattened it on that side, too. We did that a few more times and then he said, "Now fold it over so you have one of your hands covered in dough, and you're going to throw it back and forth. Like this." He showed me what he meant, and as he did he said, "Left hand. Right hand. Left hand. Right hand. And do it as hard as you can. Got it?"

I held my breath as I held out my left hand sandwiched in the dough and tried to toss it into my right hand. The dough bunched up, and I almost dropped it. "Ack!" I said. "That's hard."

"Faster. And really smack it against your hand." He showed me again how to do it. Why did it look so easy when he did it? "The quicker you do it, the easier it'll be, I promise."

So I tried again and threw it, hard and fast into my other hand. "Great!" he said. "Keep going."

I fumbled the dough a couple of times but somehow managed to keep it from falling out of my hands completely. I couldn't believe how much the wedges had grown from when we'd started.

"Okay, you know what comes next, right?"

"Sauce?" I asked, hoping it would be just that easy.

He laughed. "Nope. We haven't tossed it yet, Lindy. We gotta toss it."

"Like, in the air? But I don't think I can do that."

"Sure you can. Watch me. Put both of your hands underneath the crust, and all you have to do is throw it up and catch it. I'm gonna spin mine when I throw it, but you can spin it once it's back in your hands, before you toss it up again."

He tossed it up and caught it. He did it a second and third time. "Now you try!"

At first, the dough hardly left my hands. But he kept saying, "Higher, Lindy. You gotta get it higher! You want your pizza pie to taste good, right?"

I don't know what came over me, but suddenly, I decided to just go for it. To throw it as high and as hard into the air as I could. Both Harold and I watched it go up, up, and up before it started to come down—a pizza falling from the sky. I held my hands up to catch it. But they weren't centered, and so they only caught the edge of the dough, and I couldn't hang on. That beautiful pizza crust that took, like, fifteen minutes to make fell straight to the ground with a soft thud.

Pizza
An acrostic poem by Lindy Mackay

People don't realize how hard
It is to make a
Zippy pizza with
Zero mistakes but I think it's like
Asking an elephant to walk across a balance beam.

Chapter 14

SLICE: A SERVING OF PIZZA

(USUALLY REFERS TO PLAIN CHEESE)

Harold tried to make me feel better. He said it happens to everyone at one point or another. But I still felt bad, and silly for throwing it so high and thinking I could make it work. We threw my crust into the garbage, and together we worked on the perfect, beautiful crust he'd made. After we placed it on one of the wooden pizza paddles with the long handle, we put sauce and cheese on it, and he helped me place the pizza in the oven to bake.

"Great job," he told me as he raised his hand for a high five.

"I better not," I said. "I might miss."

His brown eyes sparkled as he laughed and laughed. "You know what, Lindy? You're all right. And anytime you want to come back here and try again, you're more than welcome, okay?"

"Thanks," I said, even though I wanted to eat our pizza, get out of there, and never show my face at Joe's again. I took off my apron and handed it to him. "While it's baking, could I use the restroom, please?"

"You bet."

I grabbed my bag and went into the small bathroom. Once I'd closed the door and locked it, I leaned up against it and pulled my notebook out. I didn't really have to go, I just wanted a couple of minutes to myself before I faced Vivian and Tyler. I doodled a little bit, thinking about my pizza-pie disaster before I decided to try an acrostic poem, something we'd learned about in second or third grade. Of course the word *pizza* would have to have the letter z twice, but I made it work. I didn't even have to find a way to put the word *zebra* in there.

Before I left, I washed my hands and checked myself in the mirror, which was a good thing because I had flour smudges all over my face. I cleaned myself up before I finally returned to the kitchen, also known as the place where Lindy Mackay's crust hit the dust. Literally.

"Your pizza needs a couple more minutes," Harold told me. "You want to go wait with your friends?"

"Sure," I said.

Vivian and Tyler were standing in a corner, waiting for me (the place is too small for chairs and tables) and I wondered if they'd found a spot where they'd been able to watch me in the kitchen. I glanced behind me, but I couldn't tell. I decided I'd just ask and get it over with.

"Did you see what happened?"

Vivian shook her head. "No."

I looked at Tyler and held my breath. Maybe he'd seen and she hadn't. "See what?" he asked me.

So they hadn't seen my epic pizza-crust fail. Now I had to decide whether or not I should tell them. Harold might say something to them if I didn't so it seemed there was nothing to do but own up to it.

"I dropped the crust." But as I said it, they didn't look too concerned. "Like, onto the floor?"

Tyler grimaced. "Oh no. When you were tossing it?"

"Yes. I threw it too high, and when it came down, it wasn't centered, and I just, I lost it. But don't worry, we'll still get pizza. We made one with Harold's crust. It's in the oven now."

"Well, I'm sure you're not the first," Vivian said. "Things don't always go smoothly the first time or two, you know. We get better with practice. Not perfect. No one's perfect. But better."

Before I could respond, Harold approached with a box in his hand and a smile on his face. "Here's the prize for your hard work."

Vivian took the pizza out of his hands. "Thank you for your generosity."

"Yes," I said. "Thank you."

"My pleasure." He looked down at me. "It was fun working with you, Lindy."

"Fun*ny*, maybe," I replied.

Harold shook his head and smiled as he wiped his hands on his apron. "What's your next adventure going to be?"

"We'll eat some pizza," Vivian replied, "and then we're off to a bakery. Figure we'll get the cooking and baking done all in one day."

Another kitchen? I wanted to run and lock myself in the pizza place's bathroom and never come out. Okay, gross, I take that back. What I *really* wanted to do was run home to my safe room that made me happy with its books and butterflies, and absolutely no oven in sight.

While I was trying to figure out if I could pretend to suddenly be sick, Tyler opened the box and pulled out a slice. "We better eat, Lindy. Don't want you falling down on the job later."

"I'm not very hungry," I said softly.

"I better get back to work," Harold said. He looked at Tyler. "I forgot to get you guys some napkins. Follow me to the counter, and I'll show you where they are."

One of the tall tables where people stood eating their pizzas had just opened up. Tyler placed the box there, threw his slice of pizza into it, and then followed Harold to the front counter, both of them weaving through the line of people.

Vivian and I moved over to the table. I stared at the cardboard box, wondering how many pizzas they made every day. Two hundred? Three hundred? A thousand? And I hadn't managed to make even one.

"Lindy?" Vivian asked. "What's the matter?"

"I really don't think working with food is for me," I told her. "Can we just go home?"

Her face drooped like a daisy left in a vase without any water. "You don't even know where we're going. It's called Milk and Cookies, and they make the most delicious cookies. And the people who work there are incredibly kind."

Tyler came back with napkins and must have sensed we were in the middle of a serious conversation. "What's going on?"

"I guess Lindy is feeling like she might be done for the day."

"Okay," he said as he grabbed his slice and took a bite. After he chewed and swallowed, he looked at me. "It's really good."

"I wish you could have gone back there, too," I said. "I feel bad."

"Nah," he said, wiping his mouth with a napkin. "You shouldn't. At first, I wasn't sure how this whole thing would go, but now? I'm kind of excited to see where Grandma takes us and what you'll be doing. Are you sure you don't want to go to the next place?"

"I'm sure."

"You know," Vivian said, "as I consider what I had planned for today, it occurs to me I may have underestimated you, my dear Lindy. I need to think bigger."

"Bigger?"

"Yes. Absolutely. So let's take you home because that's what you want to do, and next Saturday, I'll make it up to you. What do you think?"

"I guess?" I wished I could be more confident, but what if I failed again? Still, I couldn't really say no. I needed her and Tyler to help me with this project.

Vivian's eyes were warm and kind. "It's one little misstep on this journey of yours. That's all."

I nodded. "Okay. Home for now, and next weekend, we'll try something else."

"But can't we eat our pizza first?" Tyler said, finishing off his first slice and reaching for another one.

"Of course we can," Vivian said. "Lindy, are you sure you wouldn't like some?"

Maybe I hadn't made the crust, but I'd helped with everything else. And it looked *so* good. I smiled. "Well, maybe just one piece."

No Pressure or Anything

A poem by Lindy Mackay

Be kind.

Be good.

Do good.

Do it well.

Give it your all.

Give your best.

The world needs your best.

The world is waiting.

No more waiting.

No more demands, please!

Chapter 15

SCHLEP: SLOG. NOT-FUN TRAVELING, USUALLY BY FOOT.

When I got home, I heard them before I saw them.

"Honey, that's not progress. Progress is real live reservations. Dates where people are staying here and have given you a credit card number to hold their spot. How many of those do you have?"

"I disagree, Kevin. It's like you expect them to magically happen, and it doesn't work that way."

"But—"

I slammed the door to our apartment and said, "I'm home!" I was loud. Very loud. Too loud. But I didn't care. As long as they stopped the arguing.

"Be there in a minute, sweetie," Mom called out.

They were probably continuing the discussion with hushed voices in their bedroom with the door closed. Well, fine. At least they weren't yelling at each other.

I went to find Davis, but he wasn't in his room. It was a little after three, and his game started at four. I realized that's probably where he was, but why wasn't Dad with him?

Once in my room, I shut the door and went over to the window seat. I wrote in my notebook, waiting for Mom to come. A minute passed. Then five minutes. Ten. Twenty. After I finished a poem, I slammed it shut and started pacing. Were they still arguing? I could imagine both of them getting angrier and angrier, their faces red and their eyes narrow and cross. It made my stomach hurt.

My phone buzzed, so I pulled it out of my pocket.

I had a text from Tyler. I'd given Vivian and Tyler my phone number so we could easily make plans for next weekend.

Tyler: What are you doing?

Me: Nothing.

Tyler: I think you need cheering up. Want me to bring Odie over?

Me: Yes! I'll meet you at the front door.

Just then, there was a knock on my door. I went over and opened it. It was Mom.

"Sorry I didn't come say hi to you sooner. Your dad and I were talking. How'd it go today?"

"Can I tell you later? Tyler is bringing Odie over for a little while."

"Oh, sure." Her forehead wrinkled. "Wait. Do you mean he's bringing him up here?"

"Yes. Please don't be scared. Odie is really nice. Like, the nicest dog you've ever met. And we can hang out in my room. You won't have to deal with him at all."

"Okay. I guess that's fine."

I started to walk past her when I remembered Davis. "How come Dad didn't go with him to the game?"

"He called from work and said he was tired. Asked if Frannie might be able to come over and take him. So I asked her, and she was happy to do it."

"I bet Davis wasn't very happy," I mumbled as I walked out.

"What was that?"

"Nothing. I have to go downstairs and let them in. Be right back."

"Okay. I'll be in my room, working."

In the family room, Dad sat on the sofa with the remote in his hand, channel-surfing. I stopped and stared at him, because this was highly unusual behavior for my father, who always seemed to be doing *something*.

"Dad?" I asked.

"Hm?"

"You okay?"

"Fine. Just tired." He looked at me. "You going somewhere?"

"Tyler and Odie are coming over. Mom's fine with it."

"Great." He went back to the television.

As I walked downstairs, I couldn't shake the uneasy feeling I had. Another argument. But not just that, Dad had skipped Davis's game. Why? He loved watching Davis play. Had he wanted to be alone with Mom for a while so they could talk about the inn without us around?

I must have looked worried when I opened the door for Tyler because the first thing he said to me was, "Wow, you really do need cheering up."

As I bent down and petted Odie, I said, "Why'd you think I needed cheering up?"

"You were really quiet on the way home. You know, Lindy, it was just a pizza. Like, at least you didn't catch your hair on fire. Or grate your knuckles instead of the cheese, dripping blood everywhere."

I cringed. "Yeah. But who knows what might have happened if we'd gone to the next place. Blood might have been a real possibility. Come on. Let's go upstairs."

I stepped aside and let Tyler and Odie into the entryway.

"Heel," Tyler told Odie. I turned around and watched as Odie walked right alongside Tyler, his big, fluffy tail wagging back and forth.

"You've trained him so well," I said as we walked up the stairs together.

"Well, he's a great dog to work with. That makes it pretty easy."

"Did you take classes with him, or just figure out how to do it on your own?"

"We took some classes. And then I kept working with him after that."

When we got to our apartment, I tried to rush Tyler and Odie past my dad, but of course my dad had to get up and greet them.

"Good to see you both again," he said as he knelt down and scratched Odie's chest. "Lindy, I'm sorry, I'm so tired I forgot to ask you how it went this afternoon. Did you go to some fun places?"

"Only one place, actually," I said.

"She made a pizza," Tyler said.

Dad stood up and gave me a nod. "Really? That's impressive." He patted his belly. "And I just realized I am starving. Think I'll go make something to hold me over until dinner."

"See ya later," Tyler said as I rushed off toward my room.

When Tyler came in, he looked around before heading toward the window seat.

"Nice butterflies," he said.

I wasn't sure if he was joking or serious.

"Thanks. You're welcome to copy my idea if you want to," I teased.

He smiled. "That's really nice of you." He looked at Odie. "Down," he said as he motioned his hand toward the floor. Odie immediately obeyed the command.

I plopped onto the hardwood floor next to him, and Odie put his head into my lap. I leaned down and buried my head into his fur. Everything inside of me went soft and warm. I've always wondered what it means to feel like your heart is melting, and as I cuddled that sweet dog, it felt like maybe I finally knew. How had Tyler known this was exactly what I'd needed? When you pet a dog, it's like all the troubles of the world disappear and what's left is a whole lot of love.

"You love dogs," Tyler said. "I can tell. How come you don't have one?"

"My mom," I said as I sat up, though I continued to pet Odie's soft fur. "She's not really a fan. She's so stressed out lately, it'd probably be good for her to have one, though."

"What's she stressed about?"

"The inn. We don't have many reservations yet. She and my dad have been arguing. I hate it."

"Sorry, Lindy. My grandma says it's better to talk about things than to keep everything bottled up inside, though. I guess that was part of the trouble with my parents. My mom was upset my dad was working so much, but she didn't say anything. And then everything just kind of . . . exploded."

"That sounds horrible," I said. I stared at his black Nike sneakers. "Are you scared?"

"Of what?"

I kept stroking Odie's fur. It was so, so soft. "That they might not be able to work things out?"

"I try not to think about it much since there's not anything I can really do about it." He slid down from the window seat, crossed his legs in the crisscross-applesauce kind of way, and sat on the other side of Odie. "Are you scared? About your parents?"

"I don't know. Maybe." I looked up at him now. "Yeah."

"I hope everything works out," he said.

Even though there wasn't really anything he could do, I felt better having told someone. "Thanks," I said. "Me too."

Suddenly, Tyler bounced up to a standing position.

"You know what? This is not what I'd call cheering you up. Do you have any music on your phone?"

I pulled it out of my pocket. "I hope you like Taylor Swift."

"Odie does; that's all that matters. Turn it on, and we'll show you." So I found "Shake It Off."

"Odie, up!" Tyler said. Odie got to his feet, and then, as Tyler put one of his hands out, Odie stood on his hind legs and put his paws into Tyler's hand. "Okay, dance, Odie. Dance!"

Tyler let go and we watched as Odie danced in a circle on his two hind legs.

I laughed so hard.

Tyler smiled and said, "That's better."

Fancy and Zero

A story by Lindy Mackay

Fancy, an official member of the Library Cats Club, lived the good life.

She slept at the end of the Mr. and Mrs. Parker's bed on her very own super-soft blanket.

She drank cream from a crystal glass.

And she traveled to libraries all over the country, curling up with kids and good books.

"Fancy deserves the best," Mrs. Parker would say.

Zero, an official member of nothing, slept in a doghouse. Outside.

He ate his food from a plastic bowl.

And the Doggone Good Dog Kennel was the only place Zero ever visited.

One day, Zero studied pictures of Fancy surrounded by children. He could almost feel the love coming through the picture. Almost.

If only I could be a cat, Zero thought.

And so, he tried his best.

While Mr. Parker read his favorite magazine, Zero jumped on his lap, like Fancy. Mr. Parker put an end to that.

Zero tried sleeping at the end of the Parkers' bed, like Fancy. Mrs. Parker put an end to that.

The poor dog even tried climbing a tree, like Fancy. The tree put an end to that.

When it was time for another library trip, Zero squeezed into Fancy's travel crate and wouldn't budge. The Parkers got the hint.

On the plane, Fancy got a window seat.

"Fancy deserves the best," Mrs. Parker said.

Zero got stuck between some luggage.

At the library, Fancy was greeted outside and given a special welcome and nametag. Mr. Parker tied Zero to a tree and left him there, alone. Zero stared at the library. Sadness gurgled inside of him until it finally came gushing out.

"Yowwwwwwwww," Zero howled.

The bookshelves rattled. The kids dropped their books. And Fancy bolted outside to see what was wrong. But then a very big dog in search of a very fluffy toy snatched Fancy off the ground and ran.

Zero watched. He thought of the spot on the Parkers' bed. It could be his.

He thought of the cream in the crystal glass. It could be his, too.

He thought of the kids at the library and how maybe a dog could be just as good as a cat.

Fancy looked back at Zero with her scared green eyes. The children ran outside and one of them yelled, "We love you, Fancy. Please come back!"

Of course Fancy deserved the best. Zero knew in his heart he was the best dog to save her. So he pulled on that rope. He pulled and he pulled until finally the rope broke free so he could run after Fancy. He lunged at the very big dog, and when he did, Fancy was tossed to the ground.

The big dog ran away, and Zero and Fancy waited patiently for the Parkers to come get them, which they did as soon as they discovered what had happened. Mr. Parker scooped up Fancy. Mrs. Parker scooped up Zero. The dog licked the woman's face.

"That dog's a hero!" one child shouted.

Mr. Parker laughed. "Zero the hero!"

"We love you, Zero," another child yelled.

The Parkers finally got the hint.

"Zero deserves the best, too," Mrs. Parker said.

Back home, things changed. Zero got his very own super-soft blanket. He ate his food from a crystal bowl. And best of all, he became an official member of the Library Cats AND Dogs Club.

Chapter 16

ORDER IN: GET FOOD DELIVERED

(ANY KIND YOU CAN THINK OF!)

After we played with Odie for a while, Tyler left and I wrote a story about a dog, since I had dog on the brain. Well, okay, the story is about a dog and a cat, but mostly about a dog that wants to be loved as much as the cat.

When I finished, I was thrilled with how it turned out. It'd been a couple of hours since I'd last seen Mom and Dad, so I walked out to the family room, starving, wondering when the Chinese food would be delivered. It was so strange, though—it was like time had stopped inside our apartment. Dad still sat in front of the television.

"Dad, where's Mom?"

"At her desk, I assume."

"But it's dinnertime. Past dinnertime. Shouldn't Davis be home soon? Shouldn't we be getting ready to eat? Aren't you hungry?"

He sat forward, blinked his eyes, and pulled his phone out of his pocket. "It's not that late, is it?"

What was even happening? It was like they'd forgotten they had kids or something. I turned around and marched toward my parents' room. When I opened the door, I was about to say the same things I'd just said to Dad, but Mom wasn't at her desk. She was asleep on her bed. So that's why we weren't getting ready to eat and why no one was checking to see if Davis was on his way home yet.

I quietly shut the door and returned to the family room. "Mom's asleep," I told Dad.

"I just texted Frannie," he said as he got to his feet. "They'll be here in a few minutes."

I flopped down on the sofa and put my head in my hands.

"Lindy? What's wrong?"

How could I explain it? Nothing was wrong, and yet nothing felt quite *right*, either. It reminded me of the time the four of us got stuck at the top of the Ferris wheel at the Dutchess County Fair last year. We hadn't known how long we'd be up there—could have been five minutes or five hours. More than being stuck, it was the not knowing that had kind of freaked me out.

How long was this stuff between my parents going to last? What if Mom did everything she could think of, and still couldn't get enough reservations to make Dad happy? Then what? Would we have to move again?

"Lindy?"

I sighed and lifted my head. "I'm hungry, that's all. Do you need help figuring out what to order? Or should we wake up Mom?"

"No," he said. "Don't wake her. I guess I'm not the only one who felt exhausted today. Shall we have dumplings delivered again from Dumpling Kingdom?"

"Yes, please."

"Okay. I'm on it."

He sat down next to me and pulled out his phone just as the front door opened. Davis bounded in, Frannie right behind him.

"Dad, guess what?"

"What?"

He didn't even look up, just kept scrolling on his phone. Like he didn't even care why his son was excited.

"Did you guys win?" I asked, trying to match my brother's excitement.

"We did, but that's not the best part. I hit a home run!"

I jumped up and gave him a hug. Davis only let it last about a microsecond, because, you know, I'm his sister and there's nothing cool about hugging your sister. Still, it was more than my dad did. "Dad, isn't that great?"

Dad smiled. "Way to go, big man." He held out his hand for a high five, and Davis slapped it.

"I wish you'd been there, Dad. It went over the right fielder's head and then when he threw it in, the second baseman missed the catch. Which meant—"

"You kept running," Dad said. "Did they try to tag you out at home plate?"

"Yeah, but I slid and they missed."

"It was very exciting," Frannie said from the doorway.

"It sure sounds like it," Dad said. "Thanks again for taking him."

I kept waiting for Dad to say how sorry he was to have missed it, but he never did.

"My pleasure. Is Mrs. Mackay here, by chance? I'd like to speak to her about next week's schedule."

"She's sleeping," Dad said. "Can I have her call you tomorrow?"

"Sure. That'd be fine. I'll be off, then." She looked at Davis. "Congratulations again, young man. I hope you all have fun celebrating. Good night!"

We all said good-bye, and after the door had closed, Davis asked, "Can we do something fun, Dad? Please?"

"I was just about to order some dumplings. How does that sound?"

"But we eat Chinese food almost every Saturday night," he said. "Can't we do something special?"

Just then, Mom appeared, yawning as she walked toward us. "What's going on?"

"I hit a home run," Davis said. "Sorry if we woke you up."

The good news seemed to shake her awake a little bit. Her eyes got big and wide, and she looked genuinely happy. "Davis! That is so exciting! Of course it has to be the one time neither of us could make it."

"Well, you could have made it, but you didn't," I said. "Don't you wish you'd gone?"

Maybe I was being kind of bratty, but I wanted them to realize they were being selfish, letting other stuff get in the way of family stuff.

"Yes, I do," Mom said. And that's all she said about that. Dad ignored me altogether. I felt like a piece of dirt they were trying to shove under a rug or something. "Should we go out to celebrate? Kevin, what do you say?"

Dad held up his phone. "I was about to call in an order for food. I'm not sure I'm up to going anywhere. I think we have a cake mix and some frosting in the pantry. Lindy, you want to make a cake for dessert?"

Okay, I definitely did not want to do that. I'd had enough time in the kitchen for one day, thank you very much. Lucky for me, Davis likes to bake a lot more than I do. "I'll do it! Can I, Mom? And can I put the *whole* can of frosting on the cake when it's finished? Please?"

We all laughed. "I wouldn't want it any other way," Mom said. "Come on. Let's get that going while Dad takes care of dinner."

After they'd gone, Dad kind of scowled at me. "You didn't need to rub it in like that, Lindy. Of course we feel bad we missed the home run. But trying to make someone feel bad when there's absolutely nothing that can be done, it's not very nice. Do you understand?"

"Sorry," I said, staring at the red-and-black area rug that covers the family room floor. "I felt bad for him, that's all. Sometimes it feels like . . ."

I wasn't sure what I wanted to say next. Or if I should say anything at all.

"What?" he asked as I looked over at him. "Feels like what?"

"Like we're stuck on top of the Ferris wheel again."

He blinked his eyes a few times and then took off his glasses and rubbed the bridge of his nose with his fingers. "What in the world are you talking about?"

I shook my head. "Never mind. Can you make the phone call, please? I'm starving."

"That I can do, yes."

He went back to his phone. And I went back to my room, alone.

Breakable

A poem by Lindy Mackay

Sometimes
it feels like
I'm floating around
in a big, clear bubble
looking at people
floating around
inside
another big, clear bubble
and if I'm not careful
we'll bump
into each other
and
POP

and then what?

Chapter 17

THE MET: THE METROPOLITAN MUSEUM OF ART

Davis and I went to an art camp the following week in Brooklyn. Talia's mom signed her up, too, so it was fun hanging out with my friend all week. We ate lunch together every day and laughed at all her funny Rudy stories. She noticed my key necklace one day and asked about it, so I told her about Vivian and Tyler and how they were trying to help me unlock my secret talent.

"What have you done so far?" she asked.

"Made pizza very, very badly."

"There's no such thing as bad pizza," she said.

"There is when you drop the crust on the floor you're standing on."

"Oh," she said, trying not to laugh. I told her she could laugh since I'd already decided I'd stick to only *eating* pizza from now on.

The art part of the camp, though? Fun is not the word I would use to describe it. Let me try to find one.

Challenging?

Sad?

Completely and totally frustrating?

Four words, but yep, that about sums it up.

My mother has told me and my brother a few different times that it's good to challenge ourselves—to try new things and to struggle and to watch ourselves improve because . . . well, I don't remember why, really.

So every day when I left frustrated with myself, I'd tell myself it would get better. That the more I practiced, the better I would get. During our week at camp we did portraits, a couple of still-life paintings, and some landscapes. My self-portrait looked like something a three-year-old would do. I drew my nose three times bigger than my eyes and mouth. My mother told me she wanted to have it framed. Framed, to hang on the wall! I told her if she did that I would have to move out and live somewhere else because I could never, ever talk to someone who came over to our apartment and saw that horrible painting.

"You're being too hard on yourself," she said as we looked at the artwork I'd brought home that day.

"You're being too nice because you're my mom," I told her. "It's not good. At all. And it's okay to say so."

"Honey, what if I like it because *you* made it?"

"Then you can stick it away in a drawer and keep it. But I'm too embarrassed to have other people look at it. I'm not a good artist, and you can't really make me change my mind about that."

"Like I've said before, I believe everyone is an artist," she said. "Some just need more time and practice."

"But what if I don't really like painting or drawing? What if it doesn't make me happy, only stresses me out because everywhere I look, someone else's art is better than mine?"

She thought about that for a minute. "Hm. Well, maybe you shouldn't look around. Have you ever heard that saying—comparison is the thief of joy?"

I hadn't heard it before. I had to think for a second about what it meant, and then, as if she could read my mind, Mom explained a little more.

"There will always be someone who can do it better," she told me as she picked up the painting. "Don't focus on that because it will only bring you down. Focus on what you've accomplished. Be thankful for what *you* can do. Do you know I have one of these self-portraits that you did in first grade?"

I let out a little gasp. "You do?"

124

"Yes. Let's go look. I bet you'll be amazed at how much you've improved since then."

And she was right. I had gotten better. In the first-grade portrait, my ears looked like big, round wings. Why had I drawn them that way? I wondered. Was that how I had seen myself? But that wasn't the only problem. My face was crooked, and my head very pointy. I also didn't attempt a single bit of shadowing like I'd done this time.

She put her arm around me and gave me a little squeeze. "It's really not so bad, Lindy. We are our own worst critics. Believe me?"

I nodded because it seemed like that was probably true. But there also wasn't anything she could say that would make me magically love my latest self-portrait.

Random Thoughts

I have a question. And I know you can't answer me because you are a notebook and notebooks don't talk, unfortunately, but I'm going to ask you anyway. How am I supposed to not compare myself to other people? Seriously, how? I scroll through Instagram and all I can think is:

She's cuter than me today.

She's funnier than me.

I never get that many likes when I post a selfie.

It's like the world is set up to make us compare ourselves *to other people. I wonder if it was different a hundred years ago, before the Internet. When life was a lot simpler. Or maybe farmers looked across the field and thought,* Well, gosh darn it, his corn is taller than mine.

Maybe that's just what humans do. Maybe we can't help it.

Except we are the smartest creatures on earth. We have brains. We should be able to help it.

Shouldn't we?

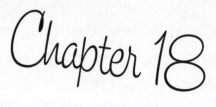

Chapter 18

TIMES SQUARE: TOURIST TRAP

On Saturday, I waited outside the brownstone for Vivian and Tyler just like I had the week before. Vivian had texted me a few days ago to tell me we'd need to meet up in the morning instead of the afternoon, though she didn't say why. It worked out perfectly because Mom had told me I could ask Nora to sleep over Saturday night and we were expecting her around four o'clock that afternoon.

This time I'd decided to dress casually and comfortably, and I was happy to see Tyler had on shorts, too. It looked like the weather was going to be perfect—sunny but not too hot.

"Hello, Miss Lindy," Vivian said. "And how are you this fine morning?"

"I'm pretty good," I said.

"Hope you had a nice week. We've been busy with all kinds of fun outings."

"We saw *Matilda*," Tyler said as he pulled a pair of black sunglasses out of his pocket and put them on. "And since it's been sunny, Grandma bought me these shades. Do you like them?"

I smiled. "Yeah. When we go swimming you can wear them to the pool. Just take them off before you jump in. Pretty sure it's hard to keep them on your head when you do that."

"So, Lindy, are you ready for your next adventure?" Vivian asked.

"I hope so," I said as I nervously fiddled with the thin ruffle at the edge of my pink shirt. "Will you tell me where we're going, or do we have to wait until we get there again?"

"I think I feel better waiting. I'm afraid if I tell you beforehand and you don't like the idea, you'll try to convince me to change our plans. And I truly believe you don't know how you feel about something until you give it a try. Okay?"

"Okay."

"You're such a good sport, you know that?" she said as we took off toward the subway.

"I'm trying," I said. "It's hard, though. Do you think you know right away that you've found *the* thing, or does it take time?"

"Hm. That's a good question. I think it can go either way. Sometimes the degree of difficulty can shadow everything else. But as we practice and it gets easier, we often discover we do enjoy it."

We walked past a coffee shop with a line of people waiting to get in, the smell of coffee hanging in the air. "When I was learning how to train Odie," Tyler said, "it was pretty frustrating at first. But we both got better at it over time."

"He's such a good dog," I said. "And you're really lucky you didn't have to toss him into the air and try to catch him with your hands."

"Yeah, that would have been tough," Tyler said with a smile.

Vivian shook her head and chuckled. "Oh, you kids."

We got off the subway at Times Square. There were lots of tourists already, even at nine thirty in the morning, taking selfies with the flashing neon billboards behind them. Times Square is probably my least favorite part of New York City. I've never really understood why people like going there. Are huge, obnoxious billboards really that exciting? I wanted to tell them all to go see a Broadway play because *that* is exciting.

"Do you know where we're going?" I asked Tyler when we got separated from Vivian in a crowd of people.

"Yes."

"Can you give me a hint?"

"I think that would be illegal."

"Illegal? You make it sound like Vivian works for the mob or something."

When I looked over at Tyler, he wiggled his eyebrows as if to say, "Maybe she does." It made me laugh.

Vivian turned around, stopped, and waited for us to catch up, so the chance for a hint was gone. She led us toward the theater district and I felt my heartbeat quicken. We weren't going into a theater, were we? Like, it wasn't possible I'd be going up on a real Broadway stage, was it?

"Here we are," Vivian said a few minutes later.

"Here" was the Nederlander Theatre. I couldn't help wondering what I'd be doing. I couldn't act. Could I?

"Is this where *Newsies* played?" I asked Vivian.

"It certainly is. Did you see it when it was here?"

"Yes, my mom and I saw it together when I was eight or nine. I loved it."

We followed Vivian through the front doors and into the lobby where there were two clerks at the ticket windows. She went up and spoke to one and before long, a man about the age of my father with short red hair and rimmed glasses approached us.

"Hello, Vivian. So lovely to see you again."

"Paul. Nice to see you, too." She turned around and motioned to us. "I'd like you to meet my grandson, Tyler, and our friend Lindy."

"Pleasure to meet you both," he said. "We have the stage for an hour. Follow me, and we'll get started."

When I heard the words *the stage*, terror filled me. But I tried my best to press it down as I followed Paul and Vivian through some messy hallways and eventually onto the stage, where a woman sat at a piano playing a song I recognized from *The Wizard of Oz*. It took me a moment to remember the title—"Over the Rainbow." It sounded so pretty, and as I looked out at the theater, I tried to imagine what it must feel like to be up there performing for hundreds of people. Just the thought made me feel like I might lose my breakfast. It made me wonder how people ever got over the fear. It seemed practically impossible to me.

"This is Gayle," Paul said as we approached the piano. "She's a voice coach and works with a number of

Broadway performers around the city. Have you ever taken voice lessons?"

I shook my head.

Gayle stood up and came over to us. She was a tall, thin woman with beautiful dark skin and shiny black hair. I'm not sure I'd ever seen someone move as elegantly as she did. "Very nice to meet you, Lindy," she said, gracefully taking my hand in hers and giving it a little squeeze. "Do you like to sing?"

"Sometimes. But I'm not sure I'm very good at it."

"Well, let's not worry about that right now. What kind of music do you like?"

"Pop, mostly."

"Vivian and Tyler," Paul said, "shall we leave these two alone for a little while? It might be easier for Lindy that way. I'll show you some of the behind-the-scenes things here at the gorgeous Nederlander, how does that sound?"

"Cool!" Tyler said.

I looked longingly at Tyler. I wanted to go with them. I mean, wouldn't I know already if I was a good singer? Wouldn't someone have heard me and told me if that was true? Like, one of my parents, one of my friends, someone?

"See you in a little while, Lindy," Vivian said with a little wave. "Have fun."

"I'll try," I said.

Gayle laughed. "You sound like I'm leading you to a filthy dungeon filled with horrid creatures." She sat on the piano bench again. "Come here. Why don't you sit next to me? That might be more comfortable for you."

I set my bag down on the floor and took a seat on the piano bench. She started playing a popular song by Ed Sheeran. "Do you know this one?" she asked.

"Yes."

"Can you sing along?"

I shook my head. I felt too shy. I'd just met her and she wanted me to sing? I hardly ever sang in front of anyone.

"Here, I'll sing with you," she said.

She started singing, and on that stage in that big, beautiful theater, it sounded so good I just sat there and listened. When she started the song over again, I knew I had to at least try. After all, Vivian had gone to a lot of trouble arranging this for me. If she came back and Gayle told her I hadn't sung a single note, what would Vivian and Tyler think of me? I had to try. I just had to.

So I started singing. "Good," Vivian said with a smile. "Lovely, Lindy. How about a little louder?"

We made it through the whole song, and when it was

finished, she turned to me and said, "That was great! How'd you feel while you were singing?"

"Nervous," I said.

"Music brings joy to a whole lot of people," Gayle said as she played the chorus of the song again.

"I love listening to it," I said. "But performing? For other people? I just don't think I'm . . . brave enough to do that. How do people do it? How do people get enough confidence to share a part of themselves like that?"

"Mm, that is a very good question," she said as she stopped playing and turned toward me again. "I think, maybe, it's about expressing oneself. And realizing we are each born with a unique view of the world, a unique voice, and the world will be a better place if we're able to find the courage to share our gifts." She smiled. "But you know, it's also perfectly fine if you like to sing and choose to do so in the privacy of your own room."

I nodded. "Gayle?"

"Yes?"

"I'm pretty sure I'm one of those who only likes singing in the privacy of my own room. By myself. I mean, no offense."

She laughed. "No offense taken, I promise. But since you're here, in this amazing place, how about we sing a couple more songs together?"

I looked out at the theater. "I guess this might be my only chance to perform on a Broadway stage." I pulled out my phone. "My friends will never believe it. Would you mind if I take our picture?"

She started playing another song, her long, graceful fingers flying across those keys. "Not at all."

Chapter 19

CENTRAL PARK: A PARK, A ZOO, A THEATER, A POOL, AN ICE RINK—ALL IN THE MIDDLE OF MANHATTAN

Once we were back out on the street a little while later, Vivian put her arm around me and gave me a little squeeze. "So I take it you'll stick to watching Broadway plays rather than performing in them?"

I let out a big sigh and said, "Yes. I mean, that was really special and I'm glad I did it, but . . ."

"It's okay," Vivian said. "No explanation needed. All right, we better get going, we don't want to be late for our next appointment."

I looked at her, surprised. "We're doing another one?"

"It's early, right? Plus it's a beautiful day. The perfect

weather for this next one. Come along, we need to take the subway uptown."

As we walked I said, "So if it's the perfect weather, it must be something outside." I looked at Tyler. "But it can't be swimming since we don't have our suits."

"I wish it were swimming," Tyler said. The way he said it, I wondered if he was getting bored. I hoped not. This whole thing had kind of turned into the Lindy show, and I felt bad.

"The pools are open now," I told him. "We should figure out a time when we can go. Mom said there's one near us that I've never been to before."

"Just let me know and I'm there," he replied.

"And it's okay that Davis will be with us, right?"

"Yeah. Sure. Whatever."

This time, our destination was Central Park. We got off at East Sixty-Third and walked past the zoo, heading toward a section of the park I knew very well—the area where the carousel, playground, and ball fields are located. I breathed a little easier. This felt much more comfortable than tossing a pizza or singing on a Broadway stage. Because it was a sunny Saturday, the place was hopping with bicyclists, joggers, and families taking their kids out to play. It smelled like fresh-cut grass, and I loved the scent so much, part of me wished we could just sit on a bench and do nothing but soak up the sights, smells, and sounds.

Vivian led us to the Chess and Checkers House.

"Do you know how to play chess?" Vivian asked me.

"Yes. My dad taught me. But I'm not very good at it."

"I love chess. When we're finished, can Lindy and I play a game, Grandma?" Tyler asked.

"I don't see why not," she said as she looked around. She seemed to be looking for someone. "Maybe we can get some hot dogs and have a bite of lunch as well."

Tyler smiled wide. "Yes! I love the hot dogs here."

"Vivian!" a voice called out from behind us. We all turned to find an Asian woman walking toward us wearing a blue T-shirt. When she got closer, I saw *Central Park Conservancy* in the corner of her shirt.

"Hello, Darlene," Vivian said, walking toward her. They hugged, and then Vivian introduced us. "This is my grandson, Tyler, and our friend Lindy."

"Hello," Darlene said. "Lovely to see you. Tyler, we met when you were much younger. You probably don't remember. Your grandmother and I have been friends for a long time."

"That we have," Vivian said. "So I called Darlene and asked her for a favor. She helps maintain the gardens here at the park, and the two of you are going to help her with a bit of pruning today."

"We have to do yard work?" Tyler said. "But no one likes doing that."

"Ah, but on the contrary, Tyler," Darlene said with a soft voice and a smile. "I like doing it and so do all the people who work to keep the park looking its best. It's not always fun per se, but there are other reasons I enjoy it. You see, when I'm out in nature around the birds and the trees, I feel alive in a way I don't feel anywhere else. I also like it because my efforts bring joy to other people."

When she said it like that, it made sense.

"Do you like being outside, Lindy?" she asked.

I'd never really thought about it before, but I realized the answer was, "When the weather's nice, like today, I do."

"Right. It doesn't get much better than this," Darlene said. "You know, there are lots of activities you could consider that take place outdoors. Not just gardening, like we're going to do together. There's the various sports you see around here, of course, but there's also bird watching and photography."

A family with a white poodle on a leash walked by, and the poodle came up to Tyler with its tail wagging. Tyler bent down to pet it before it had to scurry off to follow its family.

"If only I could spend every day this summer trying new things," I said. "There are so many possibilities, it's pretty overwhelming."

"Yeah," Tyler said. "It's like trying to choose a place

to eat in this big city. I never thought there could be such a thing as too many choices until I came here."

Too many choices. There was something about this conversation that gave me a funny feeling in my stomach. Like this was important somehow. But I couldn't figure out why. While Tyler, Vivian, and Darlene talked about their favorite restaurants, I pulled the notebook out of my messenger bag and wrote the words: *Too many choices*. I'd have to think about it later, when I was alone.

"All right, you kids ready? Let's go get you some garden tools so we can get to work."

Tyler and I looked at each other like, "There's really no way to get out of this now." Vivian had said she needed to "think bigger." Well, it doesn't get much bigger than Central Park.

"Can either of you guess how many trees are in the park?" Darlene asked as we walked along the pathway.

"A thousand," Tyler said.

I looked around. It had to be more than that. "Five thousand," I guessed.

"There are twenty-six thousand trees that grow here," she said. "Isn't that amazing?"

Wow. It really doesn't get much bigger than Central Park!

The Tree

A concrete poem by Lindy Mackay

The tree
Small, short, large, tall
Giving life to those who need it
Offering shelter to those who seek it
Providing nourishment to those who crave it
In wind, in rain, in snow, in sunshine
Standing proud and tall and true
Always strong
Gift to
All
Gift of
Life
Gift of
The earth

Chapter 20

OFF-LEASH: TIMES WHEN IT'S OKAY TO LET YOUR DOG RUN IN THE PARK

Working in Central Park was . . . interesting. We pruned bushes and pulled weeds, and within the first five minutes, I decided living in an apartment with a simple courtyard is definitely the way to go. Once we were finished, Darlene took us around and pointed out some of her favorite plants and told us the names. I could tell she really loves what she does. And when we said good-bye and went off to get our hot dogs, I felt thankful for people like her who take care of the world around us. Because while I love looking at trees and flowers, I'm one hundred percent sure I do not want to take care of them.

After we ate our lunch, we sat on the bench for a while under a couple of big trees, giving ourselves a rest before heading home. I pulled out my notebook and wrote a concrete poem, which is sometimes called a shape poem, because the words make a shape. Tyler asked me what I was doing, but I didn't want to tell him. So I said, "Writing myself a note. I need to remember to do something later."

Vivian sat with her arms crossed over her chest and her eyes closed, her head tilted back just slightly. "Lindy?" she asked.

"Hm?"

"Have we unlocked anything of interest for you yet? Or do we need to keep looking?"

I wasn't sure what to say. Was it rude to say we should keep looking? Did they even want to, or were they tired of it? Of me?

Fortunately, I didn't have to respond because Tyler did it for me. "We definitely have to keep looking, Grandma. We'd know if she'd found something she loved."

Vivian chuckled and looked over at her grandson. "We would, would we?"

"Totally. First of all, she wouldn't want to stop doing it, whatever it was. And she'd probably glow. Kind of."

"Glow?" I said, trying not to laugh.

"Like, from happiness, you know?" Tyler said, his cheeks turning pink. "Is that weird? That I think really happy people have a certain look about them? Like they know secrets we don't or something?"

"I guess I never really noticed," I said.

Just then, a lady with a black lab walked by, and the dog walked right up to Tyler, who might actually be an unknown superhero called the Dog Magnet.

"Why do they love you so much?" I asked when the lady and the dog were gone. "Do you smell like a dog?"

Vivian wrinkled her nose. "Oh my, I certainly hope not. His mother will never forgive me if he goes home smelling like a dog."

"They're my people in a non-people sort of way," he said. "They get me."

"You're so lucky," I said with a sigh.

"Uh-oh," Vivian said. "I think someone is feeling a bit defeated. Please don't give up yet."

"I'm not. I just wish when we were born, there was an instruction sheet attached."

Tyler looked at me funny. "What do you mean?"

"Like the tag on a plant that says how to take care of it. Yours would say—this boy will enjoy water sports and animals, especially dogs. Make sure his life includes those things."

"Ah, but Lindy," Vivian said as she reached over and rubbed my back, "I think part of the fun is discovering for ourselves what we like and don't like."

I wasn't sure I agreed with that. "I don't know. It seems like a big, frustrating puzzle. Maybe if I knew what my birth parents liked to do, I'd have some hints."

"We'll keep looking," Tyler said. "But, Grandma, for next Saturday, can I help pick the places?"

Vivian looked at me. "What do you say, Lindy? You game?"

I shrugged. "Sure."

Tyler rubbed his hands together. "This is going to be good." And I hoped it would be exactly that.

When I got home, Mom was dusting the staircase, just like I'd done a few weeks ago. I suddenly felt guilty for being gone all day.

"Mom? You want me to finish that for you so you can work on something else?"

She stood up and tucked a stray strand of hair behind her ear. "Oh, honey, that's sweet of you. I appreciate the offer, but I'm about finished. It's good for me to get away from the computer once in a while. I can't seem to stay away from the review sites that talk about how wonderful other inns are. I keep looking for a secret ingredient.

Like if I can figure out what it is, all our problems will be solved."

She sat down in the middle of a step and patted the spot next to her. So I went and sat next to her. I leaned in and she put her arm around me. "Did you have fun today?" she asked.

"I'm not sure fun is the right word. I sang on a Broadway stage. It was both terrifying and amazing."

Her eyes got big and round. "Lindy! That's incredible. Did you like it?"

"I mean, I'm glad I did it, but I don't want to do it again."

She nodded. "I joined choir my freshman year of high school to try it out. It was the one and only year I did it. I never felt good enough. It seemed like everyone else had something special to offer. My teacher passed me over for solos. It was the right thing to do, I suppose. My voice was just average. It's sad, but it's hard to enjoy something when you don't feel good enough."

Before I could respond, Mom sat up straight and looked around. It was so strange, it kind of startled me.

"Mom?"

"Oh my gosh, Lindy," she said as she stood up and rubbed her hands down her jeans. "That's it. That's the problem. We can't simply be another average bed-and-breakfast. We have to find a way to stand out. We should have something really special to offer to the public!"

A chill went down my spine. I pulled out my notebook and looked at the three words I'd written down earlier—"too many choices."

"I think you're right," I said. "Earlier today, Vivian and Tyler were talking about restaurants and how there are so many in Manhattan that it can be hard to choose. You need to give them a reason to choose ours."

When I stood up, she leaned down and kissed me on the cheek. "We have to start brainstorming," she said. "We need to come up with an idea that will make people sit up and take notice of our little inn. Maybe later we can even brainstorm as a family. I bet you and Davis will have some brilliant ideas."

"Nora's coming over," I told her. "Remember?" I pulled out my phone and looked at the time. "She'll be here in about an hour."

"Oh, that's right. Well, we can do it another time." She turned and trotted up the stairs. "It has to be something really, really good."

Geez. No pressure or anything.

The Lonely Princess—Part 2
by Lindy Mackay

After dinner, Li went to her room. She remembered her father's words: "My daughter, if you can get people here, to this lonely palace, as you call it, then I will allow it. But it may not be as simple as you think it may be."

Li did not sleep at all that night. She tossed and turned, trying to figure out how to interest people in staying at the palace so she wouldn't be lonely anymore.

What do people love? *she wondered.* What interests them? What can I possibly offer that they don't have?

Oh how she wished she could visit one of the villages and talk to the people there. But without a carriage to get her there, it was a very long walk. And getting a carriage without her father's permission would be impossible.

The servant who helped Li every morning had worked at the palace for many years. Her name was Ming. She was a kind woman, and wise, too. Li told Ming of her problem and tossed out ideas to see what she thought.

"A costume ball?"

Ming shook her head.

"A fancy tea?"

Ming shook her head again.

"Do you have any ideas?"

"Let them bring children to play in the empty rooms. Provide them with all the things children love. If their children are happy, the parents will be happy."

"What a wonderful idea," Li said. "A place where they can bring those they love the most. But not only that, a place that is furnished just for them."

And so that is exactly what Li did. She filled the empty rooms with playthings. One was a room for crawling infants. Another room was for small children who liked running and climbing. And there were many other rooms for older children to play games or build palaces out of blocks.

People came from across the land to stay at the palace, and to meet the princess. It wasn't long before the halls were filled with families. It made Li so happy.

Every morning, Li chose five guests to walk in the garden with her. One day a young girl said to her, "You are a lucky princess to live in a palace with a beautiful garden. Thank you for sharing it with us."

"It is my pleasure," Li said.

And what the girl didn't know was she really and truly meant it.

Chapter 21

**THEATER DISTRICT: MIDTOWN MANHATTAN
NEIGHBORHOOD WHERE BROADWAY THEATERS
ARE LOCATED; ALSO CALLED "BROADWAY." THEATERS
OUTSIDE THE DISTRICT ARE "OFF-BROADWAY."**

Nora and I sat in my room on the floor eating bowls of noodles that had been delivered just a little while ago. I'd asked Mom if we could eat in my room as a special treat since Nora was staying over. She'd reluctantly agreed.

"I would eat these noodles every day if I could," Nora said.

"But what if someone offered you a crêpe instead?"

"Well, I could never turn down a crêpe. I guess I'd have to give my noodles to you."

"We could share," I said. "Split the noodles, split the crêpe, and then we're good."

Nora finished off the last of her dinner, wiped her mouth with her napkin, and set her bowl down. "Okay, deal."

"And now I want a crêpe," I said. "Let's go to Paris. Right now!"

Nora pouted. "I wish! Oh, that'd be so fun. But since we can't, I can make some for breakfast. I've gotten pretty good at making them."

"Great. Another thing you're good at. Can you just stop already?" I teased.

"But you got to sing on a Broadway stage," she said, extending her arms high and wide, like I'd accomplished the greatest thing in the world. I'd recapped the day for her when she'd arrived. It had been the first thing she'd asked me about.

"Yes, I sang on a Broadway stage. While sitting on a piano bench next to someone who sang ten times better than me."

"But still," she said. "That's pretty exciting. Are you sure you don't want to pursue a career in theater? Maybe you could get a part in *Hamilton* and finally get a chance to see it." She reached over and tapped her overnight bag. "I brought the sound track, by the way. Just in case you're in the mood."

I scoffed. "I'm always in the mood for *Hamilton*."

"So what do you think is next on the list of things to try?" she asked.

"I don't know. I hope it's something I'm actually good at, though. I thought this whole unlock-your-talent thing would make me feel better, and instead it's almost making me feel worse."

"Sounds like you weren't bad at pruning and weeding."

I groaned. "No, but . . ."

She laughed. "I know, I was kidding. It's almost like Vivian has forgotten that you're twelve. Hopefully, Tyler will come through for you."

"I guess I'll find out." I stood and picked up our dirty dishes. "So what do you want to do now?"

"Is anyone staying here?" she asked as she got to her feet, too. "If not, maybe we could play hide-and-seek like old times. Do you think your mom would let us?"

"She should. This place might as well get some use."

"My mom handed out some of the grand-opening coupons to friends and people she works with," Nora said. "Maybe one of them will book something soon?"

I shrugged. "Who knows? All I know is I'm tired of my parents arguing about it. I keep wondering if my dad will get fed up and leave us."

Nora looked shocked. "Leave you? Lindy, that's not going to happen."

"You haven't seen him. He's been acting so strange."

"But that doesn't mean he's going to leave," she said as she headed toward the door. "Come on. Let's go ask if we can play hide-and-seek. It'll be fun."

"Davis will probably want to play with us," I said. "Hope you're okay with that."

"I love your little brother, you know that."

"I think you mean, love to *pick* on him, right?"

She laughed. "What? Me? No way."

"Riiight," I said.

We found everyone in the kitchen cleaning up after dinner. Dad and Davis were at the sink washing and drying dishes, while my mom wiped down a counter. "Mom?" I said.

"Yes?"

"Could Nora and I play hide-and-seek on one of the floors? I wouldn't ask if anyone were staying here, but since it's empty . . ."

"So glad to see our investment is paying off in such big ways," my dad mumbled.

My mom scowled. She turned and stared at my dad. I could tell she was trying to figure out what to say. And I wanted a do-over. I shouldn't have brought up the fact that the place was empty. Not in front of Dad, anyway.

After an awkward silence, Mom must have decided it was better to ignore the comment. We had a guest, and the last thing we needed was an argument for her to witness. "Yes. You may play on the third floor. You'll need to get the third-floor key chain from my desk, though. All the rooms are locked."

"Can I play, too?" Davis asked. "Please, oh please, sweet sister of mine?"

I rolled my eyes at Nora. "Sure, Prince Charming, but no cheating!"

"I'm not a cheater," he said. "Besides, how do you even cheat at hide-and-seek?"

I didn't know, exactly. All I knew was if we didn't get some reservations soon, I wanted to find a spot to hide and stay there forever. Or at least until Mom and Dad stopped arguing.

Early Riser
A haiku by Lindy Mackay

Waiting for sunrise,
while the rest of the world sleeps,
I'm dreaming of crêpes.

Chapter 22

FOODIE: SOMEONE REALLY INTERESTED

IN FOOD AND COOKING.

THERE ARE A LOT IN NEW YORK.

Mmmm," Davis said with his mouth full of food, "thith ith tho good."

"You should finish chewing before you compliment the chef," I told him. I turned to Nora next to me at the table. "But he's right. They are really, really good."

"Thanks," she said. "I like making them. They're fun once you know what you're doing."

I had watched her while she made them, and it didn't look *too* hard. Still, I had a feeling mine wouldn't turn out anything like the ones we were eating now.

Mom and Dad walked in, both of them showered and dressed for the day, and said, "Good morning."

"She made enough for you, too," I told them. "Do you want me to get you some plates?"

Mom smiled. "I'll get them when I pour us some coffee. Did everyone sleep okay?"

"Yes," Nora said. "I love Lindy's room."

"I did until a ghost woke me up," Davis said as he reached for his milk.

"No such thing as ghosts, buddy," Dad said.

After Davis took a drink, he said, "You wouldn't say that if you saw what I saw. He stood at the end of my bed and he had a head and arms, but his body was all blurry, like a shadow. Mom, what if this place is haunted?"

"It's not haunted, honey. I bet you just had a bad dream."

"Hey, what if we told people it's haunted?" I said. "Maybe people would love it. Maybe they'd want to stay here for a chance to see a ghost."

"But I don't want to live in a haunted house," Davis said.

"And you don't have to," Mom said in her reassuring voice. "Lindy, that's really not the direction I'd like to go, but I love that you're thinking of ideas. Keep 'em coming!"

My phone buzzed. I pulled it out of my pocket.

Tyler: Want to go on another adventure? Since there's only one Saturday left until I go home, we thought you might want to do something today, too.

Me: My friend Nora is here. Can she come, too?

Tyler: Yes! Be there at 11:00.

"Mom?" I asked.

"Hm?"

"Vivian and Tyler invited Nora and me to go out with them today. Is that okay?"

"Sure. I told Faye we'd have Nora back to her house before dinner, so just make sure they know that, okay?"

I looked at Nora, who had a big grin on her face. "I'm so excited!" she said.

"That makes one of us," I teased.

"But today might be the day," she said. "You never know."

"That's the spirit," Mom said. "It's a new day, Lindy. Who knows what will happen?"

This time, we ended up at the Bronx Zoo. I felt myself relax a little because maybe we would just look at things—no cooking or singing required here. But if they wanted me to discover a deep love for hippos I never knew I had, I was a little worried they might be disappointed.

After we got our tickets, we went through the main entrance and immediately saw the African plains exhibit, where the lions, gazelles, and zebras live. We stopped and watched the lions for a minute. The female lay sunning herself on a rock, while the male sat nearby in the grass, truly looking like the king of the jungle.

Lions are so lucky, I thought. They don't worry about what they're good at—what their special talent might be. They run. They play. They roar. They attack. They eat. They sleep. It's just the way things are—they're good at living life like a lion. Why did it have to be so much harder for humans?

"We're meeting someone in a little bit," Vivian told us as she started walking up the pathway again. "Afterward we'll get some lunch and walk around and see more of the zoo."

The three of us walked slightly behind Vivian, and I poked Tyler's arm. "Okay," I said. "So I guess you're not going to have me pry a lion's head open and stick my head inside?"

"Pretty sure that's a circus," he said, "not a zoo."

"Yes," Vivian called over her shoulder. "We're saving that for next time."

"Aw, too bad," Nora said. "I really wanted to see that!"

We turned to each other and laughed. As we walked

past a food cart, the smell of fried dough and cinnamon made my stomach growl. Mom had given me some lunch money, and quite a bit, too, because she'd felt bad that Vivian had bought me lunch at Central Park yesterday. I hoped when we were finished doing whatever it was we were going to do, I could offer to get everyone something to eat.

Vivian stopped at the big wooden structure with a large green chrysalis hanging from it—the entrance to the Butterfly Garden.

"We're going in here?" Nora asked.

"That we are," Vivian said. "Have either of you been here before?"

"Yeah, but it's been a long time for me," I said.

"Me too," Nora said.

Vivian nodded. "Well, good. Lindy, Tyler said you like butterflies, so I thought we might see some up close and personal as well as talk to an expert."

Nora smiled at me. "I love this! Lindy, butterflies are totally you."

I looked at Tyler, kind of amazed he'd actually remembered the butterflies on my bedroom wall. "This is a really great idea."

"Yeah, it is, isn't it?" he joked. "Grandma should have put me in charge from the beginning."

The last thing I wanted to do was make her feel bad. I looked at Vivian. "I think you've done a wonderful job. I'm the one who can't do anything right. And now let's just hope I don't step on a poor butterfly when we walk through those doors."

"Ew. Hopefully they'll be on the flowers and not on the path," Nora said.

I gulped. I guess we were about to find out.

Chapter 23

THE BRONX: THE NORTHERNMOST OF

THE FIVE BOROUGHS

When we walked into the garden it felt like we'd walked into some kind of magical tropical forest. The place was really warm and humid, and there were plants and flowers everywhere. And the butterflies—everywhere I looked I spotted at least one, and they came in lots of different colors.

"Ooh, look at the neon-green one," Nora said, pointing to one perched atop a small glass dish of fruit. "I wonder if it glows in the dark."

A volunteer walked up and asked if we'd like a

pamphlet that showed the different kinds of butterflies that could be found in the garden. We each took one.

"There are *so* many," Nora said as she scanned the brochure. Then she looked over at me and stared. She pointed to my shoulder as she whispered, "Don't move, you have company."

Very slowly I turned my head to find a bright orange butterfly perched there like it was the most natural thing in the world.

"See?" she said. "They love you."

It sat on my shoulder for a minute before it flew off. Free to move again, I turned and read some of the signs posted throughout the garden. One said *Butterflies may give the appearance of being carefree, but they face serious challenges at every stage of life.*

I was curious about that—I wanted to know more. Like, what kind of challenges?

Vivian stepped up next to me. "I think that can be true of people, too, don't you?"

"What do you mean?" I asked.

"It can be easy to assume that other people have it easier than we do. That they've got everything figured out when we're still back here at step one, simply trying to get started. Everyone has challenges."

I thought about that. "My mom and I watched a

documentary on Misty Copeland one time. You know, the famous ballerina?"

"Yes."

"When you watch her dance, you'd never guess that she had problems with injuries. For a while, she didn't think she'd ever get a chance at the principal dancer spot. But she did it."

"That's an excellent example," Vivian said. "Are you interested in ballet?"

I shook my head. "I like watching it, but I'm not the dancer type."

"I'm with you on that." She looked at her watch. "We should probably go meet my friend now."

"Does she work here?" I asked.

"Yes, but wait until you see exactly where she works. I think you're going to love it."

We found Nora and Tyler and then walked over to a spot that allows people to look through a glass window of some kind of research room, with metal tables and stools, and a couple of large white boxes with rows and rows of cocoon-looking things inside. There was a young woman working in there, and when she finally looked up from her work, Vivian waved at her. "That's Midge," she told us.

Midge motioned to us to go around to the side where we found a door marked *Authorized Personnel Only*. We waited until she opened it and let us in. Vivian introduced us to her friend, and Midge asked us if we'd enjoyed what we'd seen so far. We all said yes, and then she told us this was where they hatched new butterflies for the garden.

"One of the things I love the most about butterflies is the metamorphosis process they go through. It's a Greek word that means 'transformation.' There are four stages of metamorphosis: egg, larva, pupa, and adult. The pupa of the butterfly is also called a chrysalis. In nature, they're often suspended on a branch. But you can see here that we have a number of them suspending from the top of this box."

She carefully slid out a tray of chrysalises so we could see them up close. "They aren't very exciting to look at, but imagine what's going on inside. Wings are being formed along with other body parts."

"It's really amazing when you stop and think about it," Vivian said.

"I can't believe that this is your job," Nora said. "Working with butterflies."

Midge slid the tray back and closed the box. She was tall and thin with dark skin and black hair pulled back into a bun. And she wore a white lab coat, so she looked like the researchers you see on television.

"People who work with insects are specialized scientists known as entomologists," Midge said. "But most also choose a specific kind of insect to focus on. People who study butterflies are called lepidopterists. That's what I am."

"Have you always been interested in butterflies?" Vivian asked.

She nodded. "I grew up in Connecticut, and my parents loved having a garden. It was important to them to have plants that would provide nectar for bees and butterflies. I enjoyed watching and learning what plants the butterflies seemed to love most. And that's one thing you could easily do, Lindy, if you're interested, is create a butterfly garden of your own. You don't need a ton of space, just enough for a few of the right kind of plants."

"The brownstone has a little courtyard," Nora said to me. "Maybe you could plant some things out there that would attract butterflies."

Midge reached over and grabbed some brochures from one of the tables. "This tells you how you can create your own butterfly garden at home."

I took the brochure, but it felt like my heart had sunk into my stomach. As much as I loved the butterflies, I really didn't think gardening was my thing. What if I planted a bunch of stuff, attracted the butterflies, only to have all the plants die later? I'd feel terrible. I think Vivian must have seen the disappointment in my face.

She said, "The other thing to consider is that they hire volunteers to work here and answer questions.

Maybe in a few years, when you're older, you could apply to work here as a volunteer. The zoo would train you and teach you all kinds of neat things about butterflies."

Now that sounded more promising, though how would it look on a high school application? *I plan to volunteer at the Butterfly Garden someday a long time from now.* Like, who would care about that?

Midge talked for a while longer, telling us about the monarch butterflies and the migration that occurs every year, not realizing I already knew some of the stuff from the research for my report. I kept looking out the window, trying to spot butterflies on the plants just outside the window. I was close and yet so far—a feeling I'd felt a lot those past few weeks. And I was really tired of it.

I fingered the key underneath my shirt. The longer we did this, the more I wanted it to fit somewhere, anywhere, before time ran out and summer was gone.

Metamorphosis
by Lindy Mackay

What if we
could go to bed,
wrap ourselves in blankets,
wish to become something special,
and wake up completely changed?
It would make going to bed
a lot more fun,
that's for sure.

Chapter 24

THEATER BUFF:

LIKE A FOODIE BUT FOR BROADWAY SHOWS

That night, after dinner, I decided it was my turn to do something nice for Tyler. Earlier I'd done an Internet search for homemade dog biscuits and found a recipe that didn't look too hard, using peanut butter and mashed bananas. Who knew dogs like bananas?

I don't know why I felt more comfortable making dog treats than I did something like cookies. Maybe because if I messed up, Odie couldn't say how bad they were—and he'd probably still eat them.

As I rolled out the dough in order to cut them with a small, round cookie cutter, I thought about how Tyler and Odie wouldn't be here much longer. Fourth of July was less than a week away, and they'd be going home after that.

How could it be July? The summer was going by too fast. I felt anxious thinking about how we didn't have much time left to unlock my special talent. I was starting to wonder if I might not ever figure it out. Maybe choosing emojis was as good as it was going to get. But that wasn't the only thing that bothered me. I was going to miss Tyler, and Odie, too. Hopefully they'd come back to see Vivian again someday soon, but who knew when that would be? I remembered the way Odie had let me love on him when I needed to. I was glad Tyler had him—anytime he was feeling down about his parents, he had a loyal friend who'd be there for him. Not everyone had that, though it'd be nice if we did.

And that's when a teensy-tiny idea that had started to form in my head when I wrote the princess story snowballed into a gigantic idea—an idea that might just save the B&B.

I put a bunch of the biscuits on a cookie sheet and stuck them in the preheated oven. I had thirty minutes before the timer would go off, so I went looking for Mom. I wanted to ask about taking Tyler to the pool one day next week, and if she was in a good mood, maybe I could tell her about my idea, too. But I couldn't find her in the apartment anywhere. Davis was spread out on the sofa, reading a comic book.

"Where's Mom?" I asked.

"She went down to the library," he said. He looked up at me. "I mean, not the city library, the library room on the first floor."

I smiled. "Yeah. I know what you mean. I'm going down there, too. If I'm not back in thirty minutes and the timer goes off, can you please take the cookie sheet out of the oven? And don't forget to use potholders."

"What are you making?"

"Dog biscuits."

"What are they made out of?"

"Peanut butter, bananas, and some other stuff."

"Yum," he said. "Can I try one?" He got on his knees, put his hands up by his chest, and stuck his tongue out, like a dog.

I shook my head. "Davis, you are so—"

He flopped back down on the couch. "Adorable. I know."

I figured there was no use arguing.

I found Mom sitting in one of the vintage wingback chairs reading *A Tree Grows in Brooklyn*.

"Hi, Mom," I said, taking a seat in the other chair across from her.

She set the book in her lap. "Hi, sweetie."

"Did you want to be alone or . . . ?"

"No, it's fine. I just didn't want to do any more work tonight. Needed a little break. And I really love how this room turned out. Figured it might as well get some use, even if it's only me."

"I love it, too. Hey, can we go to the real library some-time next week? I could use some new books to read."

"Yes, that's a good idea. I wanted to spend some time with you and Davis next week, so we'll definitely do that. Maybe go to the pool, too."

I smiled at the way she seemed to have read my mind. "Can Tyler go with us? He loves to swim, and I told him we'd probably be going soon."

"Sure. So you two are getting along well?"

"Mm-hm. But I only like him as a friend, so don't worry."

She smiled. "I wasn't worried. I'm happy you've had someone to pal around with on the weekends. It'll be kind of sad when he goes home, won't it?"

I nodded as I chewed on my thumbnail. "Yeah. I think I'm really going to miss him."

She stared at me for a moment before she said, "I'm sorry I haven't spent much time with you kids this summer. I've let my work consume me, and that's not good."

I took a deep breath and then decided to finally ask her the question I'd wanted to ask for weeks. "You and Dad aren't going to get a divorce because of this place, are you?"

Her eyes got big and round. "Lindy! Why would you say that?" She stood up and put the book on the chair, then walked over to my chair and knelt down in front of me. "Are you worried because you've heard us talking about it?"

"Mom, pretty sure it was more like *fighting* about it. And yes, I heard."

She studied me, her blue eyes so sad that I wondered if she might start crying. After a deep breath, she curled her legs underneath her and sat on the edge of the area rug in front of my chair. "No. We are not going to get a divorce. And I'm so sorry, because we should have been more careful with our conversations. The last thing I'd ever want to do is worry you. Couples disagree sometimes. It's healthy to talk through problems."

"That's what Tyler said," I told her.

Mom let out a little gasp. "You told Tyler about this?"

"He's here because his parents were having problems. I figured he'd understand how I felt. I mean, who else was I going to talk to about it?"

She kind of pursed her lips, looking not too happy with me. "Me? Or your dad? Or both of us even."

"But you would have told me everything's fine, like you are now, and how do I know that's *really* true? You might just be saying that because you don't want to hurt me. Tyler was there, and Odie, too, and it just kind of . . . came out. I mean, haven't you noticed that Dad has been acting pretty strange lately?"

"Well, he has a lot on his plate at work right now, and then there's the inn stuff that is causing some additional stress." She reached up and put her hand on my leg. "But he's okay. And we're okay. Believe me?"

I looked into her eyes, and what I saw there was a whole lot of motherly love. I wanted to believe her. "Yes," I finally said. "Still, what are you going to do about this place? We really need to think of something."

"I do have one idea," she said.

"So do I," I told her.

Mom clapped her hands before she got to her feet. "Time for a family meeting. We need to make a decision and then figure out a plan. Come on."

When we got upstairs, Mom called Dad and Davis to the kitchen table. The apartment smelled good—a little bit like banana bread baking.

"Are we having dessert?" Davis asked. "Those dog biscuits smell good."

"You're not having a dog biscuit," Mom said. "When we're done with our family meeting, we can have some ice cream. I bought a half gallon of caramel swirl yesterday at the store."

"Yum!" Davis said.

Dad came and took his seat at the head of the table. "What's going on?"

"I'd like to discuss the inn. The name of our B&B is the Chorus Inn, with a little nod to Broadway, right? Yesterday, as I sat at my desk brainstorming, I came up with the idea that we name each room after a famous Broadway play or musical. You know, the *Annie* room, the *Wicked* room, the *Phantom of the Opera* room."

"The *Hamilton* room!" I suggested.

"Yes," Mom said. "Exactly. We'll be *the* place to stay for theater buffs. I'll buy some photographs of the various theaters and have them framed. Maybe get a few more knickknacks for each room based on that room's theme."

"Julie, how much is this going to cost us?" Dad asked.

"Don't worry," I said. "She's really good at bargain shopping."

Mom crossed her hands on the table in front of her. "Thanks, Lindy. Yes, it wouldn't cost much if I shop flea markets and thrift stores. I just need to be thoughtful and creative about it all." She looked over at me. "But before we decide that's what we should do, I'd like to hear everyone's ideas. Lindy said she has one. Does anyone else have an idea about how we can make this place more interesting? More marketable?"

Dad shook his head. Davis said, "Offer free ice cream to everyone!"

"Except six months of the year, when it's not exactly hot outside, people don't want ice cream," I said.

"I do," Davis said. "I'd eat ice cream all three hundred and sixty-five days a year if I could."

"Yeah, well, you're weird," I said.

"Okay, that's enough," Mom said. "Please tell us your idea, Lindy."

"You're probably not going to like it, Mom," I said.

"Let me guess," Dad said, "you want the two of us to play free ukulele concerts every night."

"Um, no," I said. "I thought we wanted to attract people, not make them run away screaming."

Dad chuckled. "Hey, we're not that bad."

"You'll never know what I think until you tell us," Mom said.

"Okay, it's just that, it involves something you don't like very much."

Mom looked at me funny. "What?"

I wrung my hands under the table. "Dogs."

Random Thoughts

I knew she wouldn't like it, but I still wanted to try. Because I think it's a great idea and I love it! I know we'll never own a dog, so this would be the next best thing. And Mom wouldn't have to get close to any of them if she didn't want to. They'd come in, go to their rooms, and stay there until they went out with their owners. Davis and I could help walk them, too, if people wanted us to.

It's probably hard for people to find nice places to stay that take dogs. That's why I think it's a pretty brilliant idea, because it meets a need. Having rooms named after Broadway plays might be a fun idea, but that's all it is—fun. It's not like people are going to be jumping up and down to stay here because of that.

Mom said she'd think about it, but I don't think she is. I think her mind is already made up. I've been brainstorming catchphrases to go with the name of our bed-and-breakfast, and I like this one the best:

> The Chorus Inn
> A Dog's Best Friend

It's a play on words because a dog is known as man's best friend. But maybe this is another thing I'm not good at—marketing or whatever it's called. *What* am *I good at, though? That's what I want to know. The longer I try to figure it out, the more I wish I could find out a little bit about my birth parents. Maybe I'd have some clues to help me figure out where to focus.*

Sometimes being adopted feels like opening a book in the middle and reading without knowing how it starts. I can't help but wish I could simply flip to page one and start from the beginning.

Chapter 25

BROOKLYN BRIDGE: THE FIRST BRIDGE THAT CONNECTED MANHATTAN AND BROOKLYN (OVER THE EAST RIVER)

On Monday, Davis and I ran around the city with Mom while she collected items that would turn the B&B into a theater lover's dream. She seemed really excited about her idea and hadn't said another word about mine. So I let it go. I couldn't think of anything else I might say to get her to change her mind. She didn't like dogs. No, it was even worse that that. She was *scared* of dogs. It was like telling Davis we were going to turn the place into a haunted house, but he'd still have to sleep there.

On Tuesday, we did some more shopping and also went to the library. Mom let me check out as many books as I could carry in my book bag, so I came home with a bunch to keep me reading for a long time. Or at least a week.

Wednesday afternoon, as we were getting ready to go to the pool, Mom got a call on the business phone. She took it in her room, and when she came out, she had a huge smile on her face. "We have a reservation," she said. "For five nights! They're arriving on Friday and will stay through the fifth. I'm so excited! Maybe the rest of the summer will fill up after all."

And so, with our very excited mother, we went to pick up Tyler for a couple of hours of swimming at our favorite pool back in Brooklyn. Nora and her older brother were going to meet us there, too. Mom had asked Vivian if she wanted to come along with us, but she had some errands to run and figured she'd do them while Tyler was with us.

"Before we hop on the subway," I told Tyler as I handed him the paper bag, "can you take this back to your apartment really quick? I made Odie some dog treats."

"You did?" he said with a smile as he peered inside the bag. "Wow. Thanks. He's going to love these."

"I hope so."

"Yeah, they're really good," Davis said.

I gave my brother a little shove as Tyler laughed.

"I'll be right back," he said as he rushed off. A few minutes later, we were making our way to the subway station.

"Does your pool have a diving board?" Tyler asked.

"Nope," Mom told him. "I think the pools here are too crowded, and the lifeguards can't deal with jumping on top of everything else."

"Yeah, you can't even jump off the deck into the water," Davis complained.

"Why'd you want to know?" I asked Tyler. "Do you have some fancy dive you were hoping to show us?"

Tyler smiled. "No, I just like diving off boards. It's fun."

When we got on the subway, a couple of teens carrying a boom box and a microphone got on, too. As soon as the doors closed, one of them pressed play and they started singing to us. I already knew they'd sing until we almost reached the next stop, and then they'd ask for us to give them money.

Mom leaned in from the other side of Davis and said, "Lindy, it's really not a good idea to give money to people you don't know. You should always keep your wallet safely zipped in your bag, close to you."

I already knew this but I simply said, "Okay, Mom."

Every time we'd gotten on the subway this week,

she'd tried to turn it into a teachable moment. At least it was my mother and not Frannie the nanny. That would have been ten times worse.

At the next stop, the singing stopped, and the performers collected a little bit of money and got off. Now we could go back to talking again.

"Do you ride the subway by yourself at home?" Davis asked Tyler.

Tyler shook his head. "Back home we have what's called the RTA. I don't know what it stands for, but it's a light-rail system. My family has never used it much. It's different in Ohio because if you have a car, it's usually faster to just drive there. Or that's what my dad says, anyway."

Davis started talking to Mom about something, so I took the opportunity to ask Tyler about his parents. "Have you talked to them lately? Your parents? Have they said anything about . . . you know?"

"I've texted both of them almost every day," he said as he fiddled with his sunglasses, which he held in his hands. "They say they miss me, and that things are going okay. And that's about it. After that, they just want to know what I'm up to and if I'm having fun."

I tried to imagine what that must be like—to know that they were trying to work out their problems, but not be sure if they actually would or not. Did he wake up every day worried? I was pretty sure if it were me, I'd be a bundle of worry all the time. Like, one big chrysalis of worry.

"Maybe what they're going through is like the caterpillar turning into a butterfly," I told him. "You can't see what's going on, right? But I think you have to believe that what will come out of all of this will be something good."

"I hope you're right," he said.

I hoped so, too.

"At least you're here with your grandma, having a good time. And you're so lucky you have Odie with you."

"Yeah," he said. "I can't even tell you how much it helps to have him along for the trip. You know how little kids have blankets they carry around everywhere that make them feel better?"

"Yep," I said. "I had one. It was pink with a satin edge. It was like magic, the way it made me feel better."

"Dogs are like that, too."

"Soft," I said.

"Fuzzy," he said.

"Soothing," I said.

"Always there for you," he said.

"Okay, you're making me want a dog so bad I think I might cry," I said. "Quick, where's a blanket so I can soothe myself?"

He laughed. "Sorry, Lindy, but you're not two anymore."

"Don't you wish we were sometimes?" I asked.

"Sometimes, yeah. How come when you think back to when you're little, you only remember the good stuff? It's strange, isn't it?"

"So maybe twenty years from now, we'll only remember the good stuff from right now."

"I hope so," he said again.

That seemed to be one thing we were both pretty good at. Hoping.

Pool Pals

A poem by Lindy Mackay

We splashed,
we laughed,
we giggled,
we wiggled,
we tanned,
we fanned,
and when it was over,
we went home
and dreamed
and schemed
of doing it all again.

Chapter 26

SIDEWALK POEM: A POEM WRITTEN ON THE GROUND

FOR ANYONE PASSING BY TO ENJOY

Our first guests arrived on Friday. They were a couple from Kansas, so Mom gave them the new *Wicked* room that includes a candle in the shape of a ruby-red slipper and a black-and-green print of a witch flying on a broom, among other things. Mom said they were thrilled.

"We have to treat them like royalty," Mom told Davis and me that afternoon as we walked into Washington Square Park. Well, Mom and I walked while Davis rode his scooter. "Maybe they'll leave reviews everywhere. Maybe they'll tell all their friends. Word of mouth is our best friend right now. I keep looking at the other B&Bs,

checking their schedules to see how booked up they are, and it's so frustrating that we don't have more reservations. Our rates are competitive. We're in a good location if you love the West Village, and who doesn't love the West Village, really?"

"Mom, don't you remember what you told me?" I said. "Comparison is the thief of joy."

She groaned. "Oh, Lindy. You're a clever one, you know that? And you know what else? You're right. I need to stop thinking about what others are doing and stay focused on my job."

It was a really nice afternoon, not too hot, so a lot of people were out enjoying the nice weather. All around us there were people walking their dogs. I almost pointed it out to Mom, to prove to her that there were a lot of dog lovers in the world who would appreciate a dog-friendly B&B, but I decided not to. It seemed like her mind was made up.

I stopped at a sidewalk poem written in chalk and read it. I loved that someone would write a poem and then share it in a place where thousands of people would walk by every day and read it. I wondered if I'd be brave enough to share any of the silly little poems I wrote in my notebook if I didn't sign my name or anything. It only took a second for me to decide no way. Those words were for my eyes only. People who wrote sidewalk poems were a lot braver than me. And much better writers, too.

"That's really neat, isn't it?" Mom said. Davis was riding in a big circle around both of us as well as the poem on the ground.

I pointed to a star. "I like how they drew pictures for some of the words. There was a magazine we used to read at the doctor's office when I was little that had stories like that. What was it called?"

"*Highlights*."

"I loved that magazine."

She stroked the back of my head. "You are my story girl, that's for sure. You read all those library books yet?" she teased.

"Not yet," I said. "But almost."

"Guess we'll have to go back next week, then."

We followed Mom over to the fountain, where she took a seat. I sat next to her.

"Can I ride around the park?" Davis asked.

Mom pulled her black round sunglasses out of her bag. "Yes, but watch where you're going and please don't get in people's way. It's annoying."

"Okay."

Mom let out a big sigh, and after she put on her glasses, she leaned back onto her hands and turned her face to the sun. "This has been a good week."

"Tomorrow's my last Saturday with Vivian and Tyler," I said. "I wonder where we'll go."

"It's kind of the grand finale, isn't it?" Mom said. "Although you and Vivian could continue your little adventures around the city after Tyler has gone home. She'd probably love that. From the sound of it, I think she's grown fond of you."

"Maybe," I said. "But it wouldn't be the same without Tyler."

Just then, we heard someone yell followed by a kid crying. Mom sat up straight and looked around. "Where's Davis?"

I got to my feet and turned toward the commotion.

"Mom, I think it's him," I said.

We both ran over to the spot, and found my brother on the ground, holding his arm and crying. We crouched down as Mom looked Davis over.

"Are you his mother?" a guy asked, leaning down right next to us. He looked like a college kid, maybe a little older, wearing shorts and a Captain America T-shirt. He had a big dog on a leash that sat behind him.

"Yes," Mom said. "Did you see what happened?"

"I think my German shepherd scared him. He thinks it's fun to chase scooters. Some kids love it, but I guess yours doesn't. He swerved hard and bit the dust. I'm really sorry."

"Me too," Mom said. "Davis, it's all right. Come here. Let's get you up, and we'll go home. Lindy, can you grab his scooter, please?"

I waited a second for Davis to stand up, but he didn't move. "My arm," he said through the tears. "It really hurts."

"Can I see it?" Mom asked.

Davis shook his head, and when Mom reached out, he yelled, "No!" and leaned back. "Don't make me move it!"

Prince Charming had become Prince Jerkface in a matter of seconds, which told me something was definitely not right.

Mom looked at me, her eyes filled with concern. "Can you text your dad? I think we're going to have to take him to the emergency room and have it looked at."

"How do we get him there?" I asked. "Do we have to call an ambulance?"

"Do you think you can get up and walk?" Mom asked my brother.

He was still crying. He shook his head.

"The ambulance it is, then," she said. "Text your dad. I'll call 911."

This was so not how I wanted our Friday afternoon to go. And here Dad thought riding the subway was dangerous for kids.

Notes from the ER

I'm sitting here in the waiting room with Dad while Mom and Davis are getting his arm x-rayed. They're pretty sure he broke it. Which will mean no more swimming or baseball or a hundred other things. And if that weren't bad enough, of course it had to be a dog that would cause the accident. Mom will probably never go near one again. Even worse, who knows if she'll ever let either one of us go near one again.

Dad just told me the next few days I should be ready to help Mom with anything she needs.

"Like what?" I ask him.

"Helping to clean the room where the guests are staying. Helping with our meals. Helping to entertain Davis since he'll need to lie low and take it easy while he takes the pain medication."

"But I can still go out with Vivian and Tyler tomorrow, right? It's our last Saturday before Tyler leaves."

"I think it'd be best for everyone if you stayed close to home, Lindy. I'm sorry, but this is serious."

No, no, no.

This can't be happening.

I have to go tomorrow. I just have to. Tyler's picking the places now, and I have a feeling it's going to be something good. Really good.

I'm the worst sister in the world. My brother probably has a broken arm, and here I am, worrying about the silly HAT project.

Except, it's not like I can make his pain go away. Or make his arm normal again. He'll be on the couch, watching TV, getting to eat whatever he wants because Mom will baby him. And I'm supposed to suddenly become a hotel maid?

Maybe he is my little brother, and maybe it's terrible he broke his arm, but this is SO not fair!

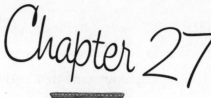

Chapter 27

OELYKOEKS OR "OILY CAKES":

THE UNAPPETIZING DUTCH WORD FOR *DOUGHNUT*

WHEN IT FIRST CAME TO MANHATTAN

The good news was that Davis wouldn't need surgery. The bad news was that he'd fractured his wrist and he'd have to wear the blue fiberglass cast for at least six weeks. Once the cast was on, he said his arm felt a lot better.

"It hurt so bad when they were x-raying it," he told us over a dinner of take-out pizza, "I thought I was going to barf all over the doctor."

"Please," I said as I set down my slice of cheese and reached for my water glass. "Stop. We're eating."

I watched as he maneuvered his slice of pizza with

only his left hand. He had to lift the piece up into the air and drop the tip into his mouth, since it was kind of floppy. I was pretty impressed that he'd figured out how to manage it in such a short time.

"Did they prescribe anything for the pain?" Dad asked.

"No. They said to give him acetaminophen for now," Mom said. "If it's not enough, then we're supposed to call and let the doctor know. I'll give him another dose before bedtime."

"Can I please have some ice cream when I'm finished?" Davis asked. "And can Lindy spoon-feed me since it might be hard to do it all by myself?"

"No, Prince Charming," I said. "You still have one good hand. I think you can figure out how to eat your ice cream. You learned fast enough with the pizza."

When I looked over at him, the look in his eye told me he'd been teasing. Ugh. Little brothers are so annoying.

Mom got up and took her plate to the sink. "Yes, you may have some ice cream when you're through. While you finish eating, I should run down and check to make sure our guests don't need any more towels or anything." She stopped midstride and said, "Oh no."

We all turned and looked at her. "What?" Dad asked. "What is it?"

"With all the excitement, I forgot to stop at the bakery and get them some things for breakfast."

Dad got up and pushed his chair in. "Most bakeries are probably closed by now, but I'll go to the market. Can you quickly make me a list of what you want me to get?"

"Thank you so much, Kevin," Mom said, rushing over to give him a kiss. "Can I text you what I need?"

Dad grabbed his keys from the basket in the center of the table, where they always put them. "Great idea. But don't forget."

Mom pulled her phone out of her pocket. "I'll do it right now, before I go downstairs."

Davis kept munching on his pizza. As I looked around at my family, I felt . . . happy. Relieved. Yes, my brother had broken his arm, but this was the most normal I'd felt at dinner in a while. It was so nice to have them focused on something besides the inn for a change. Okay, yes, it was something awful that had brought along the change, but I still felt thankful.

"Can he get us doughnuts for breakfast?" Davis asked.

Mom didn't even look up. "Sure."

Davis turned to me and beamed. I rolled my eyes. Just like I thought—they were going to baby him like crazy. But at least I'd get some doughnuts out of the deal, too. Though doughnuts would never make up for missing out on some time with Vivian and Tyler.

"Mom?" I asked.

"Yes?"

"Since Davis seems to be doing okay, can I still meet up with Tyler and Vivian tomorrow?"

"I don't know," she said. "Let's wait and see how things are in the morning, okay?"

Just then, the business phone in her room started ringing. She rushed off to answer it.

"Maybe someone else is going to stay here," Davis said.

"Maybe," I said.

I texted Nora: My brother broke his arm and that one small thing may get in the way of me unlocking my secret talent. Can you believe that?

She replied right away: Um, not really a small thing.

Me: But it's his arm, not mine. It's not fair.

Nora: Anything I can do?

Me: No. But thanks.

When Mom came out, she did not look happy. Like, instead of getting a reservation, she looked as if someone had called to cancel a bunch of them.

"What's wrong?" I asked.

She stood there, dazed. "A family wanted to stay here for a reunion at the end of this month."

"That's great!" I paused. "So why do you look like you just ate a whole jar of dill pickles?"

"Because they wanted to know if we'd take a couple of well-behaved dogs."

I almost blurted out, "I told you so!" but I stopped myself.

"Hey, that was Lindy's idea," Davis said. "You said yes, right, Mom?"

Our mother looked at him like he had a doughnut for a head. "No. I did not say yes. You really don't want dogs staying here after what happened to you today, do you?"

Davis looked down and rubbed his cast with his good hand. "That dog was just playing. It surprised me when he came running after me, that's all."

"Did you get a number?" I asked. "Maybe you can call them back and tell them you changed your mind. I mean, if Davis is okay with it . . ."

She shook her head, hard. "No. I'm not going to change my mind. Lindy, can you clean up the dishes, please? I need to run downstairs now. I'll be back in a few minutes."

"Sure."

After she left, Davis looked at me. "Dogs are a good idea, Lindy."

For once, my brother and I agreed on something.

The Little Enzo Who Did

A story by Lindy Mackay

Shimmy, shimmy, shake! Enzo did the happy dance when Sam showed him Lucy's wedding ring.

"I didn't know I'd feel this nervous," Sam said. "She'll like the ring, right?"

"Arf," Enzo barked. Right.

"And we make a great pair. Right?"

"Arf."

"Time for me to get to the church. Bye, buddy."

Enzo watched as Sam's coat got caught on the gate latch and the ring fell out of his pocket.

"Woof, woof!" Wait! You dropped the ring.

Sam smiled and waved before he zoomed down the street in his car.

Enzo snatched up the box, pushed the gate open, and raced after Sam. He ran and ran and ran. He jogged and jogged and jogged. He walked and walked and walked.

Finally, he reached Sam's car, but he didn't see Sam. Enzo looked for the church and saw it WAY up high.

He inched up the hill, but he was tired. He plopped down, right on top of the box.

"Pant, pant, pant." I can't do it.

Two ladies hurried past carrying flowers.

"Woof." Can you take the ring to Sam?

The ladies kept going.

A man rushed by carrying a camera.

"Arf, arf!" Please help.

"Get home, pup," the man said. He kept going.

A man and a lady walked by carrying a beautiful cake.

Since no one paid any attention to his barking, Enzo nipped at the lady's feet. The cake swayed this way, and that way, and this way again. And then, PLOP, it fell right on Enzo.

"Bad dog," the lady said.

"Hurry!" the man told the lady. *"Back to the bakery!"*

The church bells started ringing. People covered the hillside. Enzo barked and barked, but still, no one stopped.

Enzo looked up. He saw the big hill, the bumpy path, and the long grass. It seemed impossible. But Enzo knew he had to try. As Enzo walked, grass clung to his sticky body. He shook a prickly weed from his paw.

I can do it. I can do it, *Enzo thought as he plodded up the hill.*

Finally, he made it. Shimmy, shimmy, shake!

Piano music swirled up and around his sticky legs, past his sniffing nose, and into his icing-covered ears. Enzo spotted Sam at the front of the church, checking his pockets frantically. With his jaw locked tight around the box, Enzo rushed toward Sam.

"Stop that dog!" the man with the camera yelled. Enzo

zigged and zagged through long legs and grabbing hands until he leaped into Sam's arms.

"The ring!" Lucy said. "Enzo, you saved the day."

"Thanks, little buddy," Sam said between Enzo's slobbery doggy kisses. "You are the best dog ever."

And to prove he meant it, Sam gave Enzo a special place in the wedding.

"Sam, will you take Lucy to be your lawfully wedded wife?" the minister asked.

Sam looked nervous. He wiped his brow and swallowed hard.

"Ruff, ruff." You can do it, you can do it!

Sam smiled. "I do."

Shimmy, shimmy, shake. Shimmy, shimmy, shake!

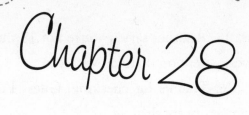

Chapter 28

**PROFESSIONAL DOG WALKER: A PERSON WHO WALKS
DOGS FOR A FEE WHEN THEY'RE NOT OUT ON AN AUDITION**

Saturday morning, I woke up early. I'd started a story the day before about Enzo the dog, and I worked on it for a long time. When I finished, I shut my notebook, satisfied. Maybe Mom didn't see dogs as good, but I sure did, and I felt happy that I'd found a way to express that somehow.

I texted Nora: Maybe I should volunteer at an animal shelter. Do you think I'm old enough?

She texted back: Great idea! I'll have Mom check. She's right here on the couch with her laptop.

A minute later: At one place you have to be at

201

least 18. Another says if you're not 18 then you have to have a parent or guardian with you.

Me: Thanks for checking. Guess I'll wait another five years to try that out.

I checked the time and couldn't believe it was almost nine. I hadn't heard anyone walking around yet, but that didn't seem right. Usually somebody was up by now.

Mom and Dad's bedroom door was shut. I went to the bathroom and quickly got dressed, brushed my hair and my teeth, and went out to the family room and then the kitchen. The box of doughnuts Dad had bought at the store sat on the kitchen counter. Then I remembered we had guests staying here. Maybe Mom and Dad went down to help with breakfast or something, even though Dad was supposed to have bought food that the guests could serve themselves.

"Hi, Lindy," I heard from behind me.

I turned around to find Davis standing there looking sort of pathetic, with his cast and his bed-head hair. He yawned.

"Hi," I said. "How's the arm?"

When he saw the doughnut box, he headed straight for it. "It's hard to sleep with a cast on. Every time I started to roll over on that side, I woke up." He yawned again. "I'm tired. And I'm sad I don't get to play baseball this weekend."

"I know. But I bet you'll get used to sleeping with it soon," I said. "Pick out a doughnut, and I'll pour you a glass of milk."

"Where's Mom and Dad?" he asked as he tried to get the lid off of the box. I reached over and helped him before I stepped over to the refrigerator to get the jug of milk.

"Sleeping, I guess," I said.

"That's weird," he said.

I turned around and watched as he chose a marble bar, which is half maple bar and half chocolate bar. No surprise, really. It was the biggest doughnut in the box.

"Here," I said, reaching up and grabbing a plate. "You'll need a napkin, too."

After he had everything, he went to the table, and I followed along with his milk.

"I'm gonna go see if they're in their room," I told him. "I'll be right back."

When I got to the closed door, I started to knock, but then I heard Mom and I stopped. She was crying. Dad was saying something to her, but I couldn't hear what it was.

They'd probably been fighting again. I tiptoed away so they wouldn't know I'd heard them. Davis had already devoured half his doughnut.

"Geez, dude, slow down or you'll make yourself sick."

"It's so good," he said before he took a swig of milk. He looked at me. "What's wrong? Are they in there?"

"Yeah," I said. "They're talking. We'll just leave them alone. If you need anything, I can get it for you."

"Aren't you going to have a doughnut?"

"I'm not really hungry."

I got up and went to the window. It was kind of cloudy, which probably meant it wouldn't be too hot. It'd be a great day to explore more of the city. Tyler had said they'd pick me up at ten so we could spend most of the day together. But it seemed impossible now. I pulled out my phone and wrote him a text:

I can't go anywhere. My brother broke his arm yesterday. I'm so sorry.

It took a couple of minutes before he replied: Oh no that's horrible! Is he okay?

Me: Yeah. He's fine. But my parents want me to stick around here.

As I waited for another reply, I heard the door open down the hall. I turned and watched my parents come out of their room, my dad first, followed by my mom. My stomach tightened as I wondered if they'd say anything to us about what they'd been discussing.

"Good morning," Dad said with a smile. He went over to the kitchen table. "Glad to see you found the doughnuts."

"Can I have another one, please?" Davis asked. "You picked out really good ones, Dad."

Clearly, a broken arm couldn't keep Prince Charming down for long.

"I think one's enough, buddy."

Mom came over and put her arm around me. "Thanks for helping him with breakfast."

"You're welcome. Is everything all right?"

My phone vibrated, but I ignored it.

"Actually, can you come over to the table? I want to tell you kids something."

My mind raced with possibilities. Was she going to tell us we had to move? That this place was a total failure and we never should have bought it? Or even worse, that she'd been wrong and Dad really was fed up and planned to leave? I stood there, frozen. I didn't want to hear what she had to say. If it made *her* cry, what would it do to us?

"Lindy?" Dad said. "What's wrong?"

I didn't know what to say. Mom came over to me again and said, "Sweetie? Oh no, you're not worried, are you? It's good news, I promise."

She walked me over to the table, and I sat down, still feeling nervous.

"Your dad and I had a really good discussion about the inn," Mom said to me and Davis. "And I realized I've been close-minded about this idea of having dogs stay here. Clearly, you kids think it's a good idea. And your dad thinks it's a good idea, too. I'm the one with the issues. And I've decided I need to work on those. So I found those people and called them back and told them they're welcome to have their reunion here."

I sat there in shock. I couldn't believe what I was hearing. "You're not scared?" I asked. "After what happened to Davis?"

"Yes, I'm scared." She wrung her hands together. "And while sometimes fear can be helpful, sometimes it can be harmful. To moving forward. To trying new things. To doing what's right. I need to get over it. Now, please understand, that doesn't mean I'll be running up to every dog that stays here, hoping to be their best friend."

"But you won't run away from them, either," Davis said. "Which is good, because if you're not careful, you might turn too fast and fall and break your arm."

Mom smiled. "Exactly."

"Can I offer to walk dogs for people?" I asked. "Because I'd really love to do that."

"I know you would," she said. "And we'll talk about that later. Right now, shouldn't you be getting ready to go out with Vivian and Tyler? It's your last day with them, remember?"

"But I thought—"

"No, I want you to go. I talked to Vivian this morning and told her you'd be going."

I pulled out my phone and checked the last text Tyler had sent me:

Grandma says your mom told her you can go. You can't chicken out now. See you soon!

I stuffed my phone into my pocket and ran to my room to get a bag, my notebook, and some shoes. This morning had turned out a hundred times better than I thought it would be.

Now, if that would only continue for the rest of the day.

Chapter 29

CHECKER TAXI: AN AMERICAN TAXI COMPANY THAT MADE THE FAMOUS YELLOW TAXI CABS WITH BLACK-AND-WHITE CHECKERED TRIM FROM 1958–1982

I ate a doughnut, a banana, and a glass of orange juice before I rushed down the stairs. I ran into our guests from Kansas as I was going down, and instantly slowed myself down.

"Hello," I said. "I hope you're enjoying your stay."

Prince Charming would have been so proud of me with my good manners.

The lady smiled at me and said, "We are, thank you."

"Joe's Pizza is really good, and it's not too far from here, in case you don't have lunch plans."

"Wonderful," she said. "Thank you."

I continued past them and out the front door. When I saw Odie sitting between Tyler and Vivian, I let out a little squeal.

"Odie," I said as I bent down and held his head in my hands. "I can't believe you get to go with us!" He was wearing a special harness I'd never seen before, and had a red bandana tied around his neck.

"All right, dear ones, we're going to hail a cab today," Vivian announced. "Dogs aren't allowed on the subway unless they're contained or helping someone who's disabled. Hopefully, we can find a cab driver willing to take us."

I stood up. "Any hints where we're going?"

Tyler raised his eyebrows. "Like we'd change things up now?"

I laughed. "Okay, okay. Let's go. Surprise me, as usual."

"We have to go quite a ways uptown for today's adventure," Vivian said. "Do you have a book to read or something to do to help pass the time?"

For a second, I thought about running back upstairs to get one of my library books, but I decided it was a bad idea. I'd already kept them waiting long enough. "No, but I have my notebook," I said without thinking. "I mean, yes, I have something to do."

"Wonderful."

It didn't take long for a cab to stop and pick us up. Vivian pulled a towel out of her bag and spread it on the backseat next to the window for Odie. He climbed up and happily sat there. Tyler climbed in next to him, and I sat next to the other window. Vivian got in the front seat with the driver, and they started chatting right away.

Tyler pulled out some comic books from his backpack. When it seemed like he was completely lost in what he was reading, I pulled my notebook and pen out of my messenger bag. I'd opened it to the Enzo story for maybe half a second before Tyler put his comic down and asked, "What have you got in there?"

"Nothing," I said. "Just doodles and stuff."

He leaned in, and I snapped the notebook shut.

"Doesn't look like doodles. Looks like words. Lots of words."

I shrugged. "Maybe."

He gave me an annoyed look. "You're really not going to tell me? What are you afraid of?"

"Nothing," I said. "It's just . . . personal. Kind of like my diary, I guess."

"Who's Enzo?"

My jaw dropped. "What? How'd you see—"

"It was right there, at the top of the page. Something about little Enzo? So who is it?"

I bit my lip as I considered how to answer. I didn't want to lie, so finally I just said, "He's a dog."

"A dog? Whose dog?"

"Well, um, he's made up, actually. I made him up."

He shook his head. "I don't understand. If it's your diary, doesn't that mean you're writing stuff that's true?"

"Well, sometimes I am. But sometimes I make stuff up. Little stories or poems, just for fun. Anyway, it's not important. It's something to do when I've run out of books to read or I'm bored or whatever."

"Lindy, what do you mean it's not important?" he asked. "I think that's really cool. I couldn't write a poem if someone offered to pay me ten thousand dollars."

I scoffed. "Oh, you could, too. It's not *that* hard."

"Can you show me one?" he asked. "Please? I'm really curious."

He fluttered his eyelashes a couple of times, trying his hardest to look sweet and innocent, and it made me laugh. Just what I needed, another Prince Charming.

"I don't know."

"Oh, come on. We're friends, right? I'm not going to say anything mean. I promise."

"But I haven't even showed it to Nora," I told him. "And she's my very best friend."

"Yeah, well, she's not here, and I am. So pick one and show me. Maybe it's your shortest one. Whatever."

I sighed as I flipped through the pages. I stopped on the haiku I'd written the morning after Nora stayed the night. "Okay, just one. I wrote this haiku last weekend, while I was waiting for Nora to wake up. You know what a haiku is, right?"

"Yes," he said. "Five, seven, five."

"Right. So I'll just read it to you. It goes, 'Waiting for sunrise, while the rest of the world sleeps, I'm dreaming of crêpes.'"

I looked at him when I finished, my stomach tied up in knots, wondering what he'd say. I regretted giving in. I shouldn't have done it. What if he hated it? What if he started laughing, or worse, made fun of it?

But that's not what happened. His eyes got really big. He looked surprised. "Lindy, that's really good. Wow."

"Thanks, but I don't know about that. It's nothing special, really."

"It is, too. Read me something else."

I nudged his knee with mine. "No. You asked me to read something, and so I did. Now go back to Spider-Man or Superman or whoever you're reading about."

"It's Batman meets Scooby-Doo," he said, showing me the cover.

I smiled. "Hey, it is."

"I want to hear about Enzo, though."

"You said to pick one, and I did. Not two. Not three. Not five. One."

"Fine," he said with a huff. "But I really think I'd like it."

With that, he went back to reading his comic book. And the rest of the way I kept my notebook shut and wished I'd gone back for that library book after all.

Chapter 30

**THE GOOD DOG FOUNDATION: THE ONLY THERAPY DOG
CERTIFYING ORGANIZATION IN NEW YORK CITY**

The driver dropped us off at the doors of a beautiful brick building. I looked around for a sign. When I couldn't find one, I asked Vivian, "Where are we?"

"This is the Morgan Stanley Children's Hospital," she said.

"A hospital?" I looked at Tyler and then back at Vivian. "What are we doing here? Please tell me you're not going to have me operate on some poor kid. I mean, if I can't even make a decent pizza, you really don't want to let me near sharp instruments."

They both smiled. "Don't worry," Vivian told me. "This one is probably the easiest by far. We're going to let you try out being the handler of a therapy dog."

I wasn't sure I was following. "Therapy dog? What do you mean?"

Vivian explained it to me. "Tyler, along with his dad, and Odie, of course, have been through special training so that Odie can come to places like this and give people comfort, affection, and a little happiness for a while. There is something pretty magical about the unconditional love of an animal, you see."

I instantly thought back to the day Tyler had brought Odie over to my house and I'd sat on the floor and cuddled with him. Tyler had known it was just what I'd needed.

Now I understood. Odie wasn't just an ordinary dog. He was a dog with a job to do. Vivian kept talking. "Therapy animals must be friendly, patient, and gentle, even with strangers. Well, especially with strangers. Odie is all those things. Tyler saw a need and wanted to do something to help people."

"There's this kid I went to school with," Tyler explained, "who didn't talk very much and had behavior problems. When they let him bring his service dog to school, I thought it was so great. All of us in his class loved that dog. And when I turned thirteen last fall, I asked my parents if there was any way Odie and I could help people somehow. And now here we are."

I stared at Odie, who sat there waiting for us to move and go inside. He was such a good dog, of course it made sense that he would do well at this sort of thing. But I couldn't deny that a part of me felt upset, too. Maybe upset wasn't the right word. Jealous. That's what it was. Because how sad was it that a dog had something he loved to do, that mattered to him, and I didn't? I tried my best to press the jealousy down as Vivian said, "Come on. Let's go inside, and you can see for yourself."

We stopped at the front desk, and I hung back while Vivian spoke to someone. A minute later, we were getting on the elevator and going up to the fourth floor. A young woman with chin-length brown hair and a slight limp greeted us. She shook our hands and told us her name was Char. She had a vest on that said *Paws for Patients*. She bent down and gave Odie a whole bunch of love and even handed him a treat she pulled out of her jeans pocket.

"I was a patient once," she told us. "Just like these kids. And now I spend time helping to bring dogs to patients because I really believe in the healing power they can provide. Now, not every patient can have visitors. So some will just have to watch from the window.

But we can still talk to them, and you'll see that the dog often interacts with the child even through the glass."

The hallway had super-shiny floors and it smelled like lemon mixed with the antibacterial spray Mom put on our knees when we were little and fell and scraped them. We walked to the first room, and Char opened the door. "Mario? You ready for a visitor?"

Mario slowly sat up and turned so his legs hung down the side of the bed. He had on a white T-shirt and green pajama bottoms. The smile on his little brown face was so big and wide it almost made me tear up. He looked about my brother's age. Of course we didn't know what was wrong with him. It wasn't any of our business. But I couldn't help but wonder about him. Knowing my brother had been able to go home after just a few hours at the hospital, it had to be something much worse than a broken bone.

Odie got right up next to the bed so Mario could lean down and pet him. After a minute or two of that, the boy bent down farther and put his cheek on top of Odie's head and closed his eyes. In that moment, Mario looked like there was nothing else in the world he'd rather be doing.

And then Tyler did something that totally surprised me. He handed me the leash. It was as if he said, "Here. You're in charge now. See how it feels."

Except I didn't want to see how it felt. Because I knew it would feel all kinds of wonderful, but it didn't matter. Maybe Mom had decided dogs could stay at the B&B, but never in a million years would she let us have one of our own. She wasn't a dog person, which meant I couldn't be a dog person. It was like taking someone who was allergic to milk to an ice cream shop. They could watch other people enjoy the ice cream, but they could never take a bite themselves. So why go at all?

I handed the leash back to Tyler. And then I turned around and walked out of the room.

Stupid Feelings

A haiku by Lindy Mackay

Ugly jealousy.
Please go away. Disappear.
You just make things worse.

Chapter 31

THE *NEW YORK TIMES*: A DAILY NEWSPAPER
FOUNDED IN 1851, USUALLY JUST CALLED *THE TIMES*.
GAVE TIMES SQUARE ITS NAME.

They came out of Mario's room a little while later. Tyler looked at me, sitting in a chair I'd found against one of the walls, and waved me over. But I threw my notebook back into my bag, tucked my legs up into my chest, and buried my face in my knees. He got the hint. Vivian followed him and Odie into another room and left me alone.

Tyler had thought I would love this. And I did. But loving something when you can't have it is really, really hard. Was I being selfish? I didn't have to think very hard to figure out the answer to that—I was acting like a spoiled brat. Here I was in a hospital where kids had it a lot worse than me, and I was out in the hallway pouting because I could never have a dog and never do the things Tyler got to do.

Except, that wasn't really true. When I turned eighteen, I could volunteer in a shelter with dogs. And when I was done with college and living on my own, I could take one of those shelter dogs with me and give him a good home. If I wanted to train him to be a therapy dog, I could do that. And I could volunteer at the butterfly garden every now and then, too, and teach people about metamorphosis, and how even butterflies have challenges.

It all seemed so far away.

But maybe right now I was like a caterpillar in a chrysalis. Maybe I had to drop pizza crusts and shake in my shoes on a Broadway stage and put the wrong flowers together in a vase because that's what it took to grow wings someday. And I just had to trust that even with me, someone who couldn't seem to figure out what she's good at, Mother Nature knew what she was doing. That someday, one year or three years or five years or ten years from now, I'd get my wings. And I would fly.

I felt a tap on my shoulder. Startled, I jerked my head up to find Vivian standing there. "Lindy? I have a huge favor to ask you. We've just met a girl, Ariel, who is a couple of years older than you. As she cuddled with Odie, she told us she likes to draw pictures of dogs. And then Tyler told her you wrote stories about dogs. And she begged us to read her one. But we can't do that because they're your stories and not ours to tell. So I'm wondering, do you think you might come in and read her one of your stories? I really think it'd make her day."

"I'm not sure it's any good," I said softly. "It's not like the pizza place, where we can just eat someone else's pizza if I ruin the one I'm making. If I read it and she doesn't like it, that's all we've got."

"So you're afraid?" she asked.

I nodded. And as I did, I remembered what Mom had said earlier, about fear. That sometimes it can be harmful because it keeps you from trying new things and doing what's right.

"You have been so brave as we've gone around the city, trying new things," Vivian said. "How do you think you've managed that even when you felt afraid sometimes?"

I thought about tossing the pizza crust up into the air. How I was scared to do it, but I did it anyway. Because I knew I would never know if I didn't try.

"It's like trying and fear were two students who were both working really hard to get their teacher's attention,"

I told her. "And the teacher was me. So I had to tell fear to sit down and be quiet because trying was the one who needed me most."

She reached out and put her hand on my knee. "I love that, Lindy. Fear can be loud and obnoxious and annoying sometimes, and maybe you feel like it won't listen to you today. So how about I take a turn at telling it to be quiet? Because I really think reading your story would be a good thing, for both you and Ariel."

I took a deep breath. It wasn't like she was asking me to share it with the entire hospital. She was asking me to share it with a couple of people. I could do that. And I realized that in a place like this, where so many people were sad and hurting, I *should* do that.

I gave Vivian a nod as I got up and grabbed my bag. Vivian led me into the room. A girl sat in a wheelchair with an IV in her arm that was attached to a bag of fluid hanging from the pole next to her. She was pale and skinny and her long blond hair, which probably used to be bouncy and shiny, was kind of flat and stringy.

"Hi," she said. "I'm Ariel."

"I'm Lindy," I said. "Nice to meet you."

She smiled, and in that moment, I knew I was exactly where I should be.

"So you write stories about dogs?"

"Well, I've written a couple. Yeah."

"I can't wait to hear one," she said.

I pulled up a chair and sat down across from her. "Okay. If you'll show me one of your drawings when we're done."

"Deal."

Odie sat next to her with his head in her lap, and she continued to pet him as I opened my notebook. "This is called 'The Little Enzo Who Did.'"

"Hey, is that like *The Little Engine That Could?*" Tyler asked.

"Yep," I said, avoiding his eyes. I couldn't think about him hearing this story or I might chicken out after all. I don't know why but it seemed easier to share it with someone I didn't know. I decided I couldn't let my brain think at all. Couldn't let fear stand up and start talking again. I just had to read it, straight through, from beginning to end. I wouldn't look at any of them. I would just read and hope that when I was finished, they would be nice enough not to laugh if it wasn't very good.

So I read about Enzo and the lost wedding ring. About how he picked up the box and carried it all the way to the church on the hill. How he ran up the hill but grew tired and had to stop and rest. And how he tried to get people to help him, but they didn't understand what he was trying to say. And so he kept going, up and up and up that hill, until he made it to the church. How little Enzo tried and tried and tried, and never gave up and saved the wedding.

When I finished, I could feel my heart beating in my chest, and if I'd wanted to, I probably could have rapped a *Hamilton* song to that loud, fast beat. I closed my notebook, and before I had even looked up, Ariel was clapping her hands. Then Tyler joined in. And Vivian. They were all clapping, and they kept doing it for what seemed like a really long time. I felt my cheeks grow warm.

When they finally stopped, Ariel said, "Wow. I wish I could write like that. Your school essays must be killer."

It made us all laugh. "I don't know about that."

I looked over at Tyler and he had a huge grin on his face. "Lindy! Are you kidding me? You don't think you're good at anything? I feel like I'm friends with a future *New York Times* bestseller!"

"But I just do it for fun. For myself."

"Yes," Vivian said. "And that's what lots of artists do for a while, as they learn and grow and practice, until one day, they finally feel comfortable sharing."

"An artist?" I asked.

"Yes," she said. "As in someone who creates art. You create stories, Lindy. You are an artist. A weaver of words."

It was strange to think of myself that way—a type of artist. But maybe . . . could it be?

There were so many things I wished I could do. Dance. Sing. Train a dog. Go to Paris. Make amazing crêpes. Spin a pizza crust in the air. But if I couldn't do those things, for whatever reasons, maybe writing and reading about them was the next best thing.

Maybe it was *my thing*.

"Oh my gosh," I said. "I've found it. I've found something I'm good at and that I love to do!" I grinned. "Am I glowing?" I teased.

"Totally," Tyler said.

"Absolutely," Vivian said.

"Okay, enough about me. Ariel, can I see your drawings now?"

"Sure," she said. "Can you get me that sketch pad next to my bed?"

"I'll get it," Tyler said.

While everyone's eyes were on Tyler and the sketch pad, I did a little happy dance in my chair.

Shimmy, shimmy, shake.

Thanks, Enzo, you awesome little dog, you.

A Magic Stick

A poem by Lindy Mackay

A pencil is a funny thing;
it's really just a stick.
But when you put it on a page,
it's like a magic trick.
The paper's blank, then suddenly
there are circles, lines, and dots.
Words turn into sentences
and POOF—
the page is filled with thoughts.

Chapter 32

THE CAPE: CAPE COD, MASSACHUSETTS

It was a beautiful August day. In five days, I'd be thirteen years old. To celebrate, Mom had let me bring Talia and Nora with us for a weekend on the Cape. My parents had rented a house near the shore, and now the three of us lay on a plaid blanket, sunning ourselves while flipping through magazines. Well, they were flipping through magazines. I was writing a poem in my notebook.

The salt-filled air, the clear blue sky, the sound of the ocean waves in the background—it was one of those moments when I wished I could magically make time stop.

Nora closed her magazine, rolled over, and sat up. "Have you guys finished your posters yet?"

"I did mine weeks ago," Talia said as she turned around and sat up, too.

"What'd you write or draw on it?" Nora asked. "I still need to do mine, and I'm trying to figure out how to combine a cello and Paris."

"You could draw a picture of you playing a cello at a sidewalk café with the Eiffel Tower in the background," I suggested.

Nora laughed. "You make it sound so easy. I think I need something a *little* simpler than that."

"I drew a big black top hat and cut out pictures of dancers from magazines," Talia said. "It's supposed to look like they're dancing out of the hat. What about you, Lindy?"

"Mine's almost finished. It's a big concrete poem in the shape of a tree, with the leaves of the tree written in green ink, and the trunk of the poem written in brown ink. Underneath the tree are flowers with butterflies fluttering around them. And I want to try to draw a dog sitting there, too."

"Wow," Nora said. "That sounds amazing." She sighed. "Okay, I think I'm going to run in the ocean and cool off. Anyone want to come?"

"I will," I said. "But let me finish this poem or I'll never remember what I was going to write."

"Hey, don't forget you wanted to get a postcard today and send it to Tyler," Talia said as she brushed some sand off the back of my legs for me. "Maybe later we can go get some ice cream and find a little postcard shop?"

I kept scribbling. "Yeah. Good idea."

"How's he doing anyway?" Nora said.

They both knew Tyler and I had stayed in touch after he left. We texted each other a couple of times a week.

"Good," I said. I finished writing the last line and twisted myself up and around so we were all sitting side by side. "His parents are still going to counseling. And everything seems to be going okay. He said it's still tense sometimes. It's not like everything is miraculously perfect, you know? But it's a lot better."

"Nothing is ever perfect," Nora said. "Even if we want it to be."

I thought of my parents and the troubles they'd had earlier in the summer. Things had gotten better at the B&B. This weekend, they'd closed the place for some deep cleaning and so we could get away for a mini vacation. The rest of August there were a bunch of reservations, which made them both really happy.

Once I turned thirteen, not only could I ride the subway, but I could also offer my dog-walking services to our guests for a small fee. Dad had made me take a couple of classes on handling dogs before he'd agreed to let me try it. I couldn't wait for next week. It seemed like I was about to enter a whole new world.

"Hey, next week, on my birthday," I said, "how about I come to Brooklyn and we go out for salted Nutella cookies at Buttermilk Bakeshop?"

"Yummmm," Talia said.

"Is that a yes?" I asked, nudging her with my elbow.

"Lindy, you should write a poem about how delicious those cookies are," Nora said.

"I could never in a million years describe how amazing they are," I said. "Like, there are no words, really. None. So I'll just stick to writing about dogs and princesses and my friends at the beach."

Talia turned and looked at me. "You wrote about us?"

I stood up and pulled on her hand. "Maybe. Come on. Let's go run in the ocean!"

She laughed and got to her feet, looking so cute in her fuchsia-pink bathing suit. "But I want to see what you wrote."

"Later," I said. "And only if you'll dance for us."

"Okay," she said as she ran out onto the sand and did a beautiful split leap right there.

Nora stood up and said, "Oh, come on. That's so easy. Look, I can do it, too."

She ran and leaped into the air. Except her toes weren't pointed and her legs weren't straight, and she landed far to one side and fell to the ground in a fit of giggles. We all knew she'd been joking when she said it was easy.

"Your turn, Lindy," Talia said, motioning for me to come toward them. "Come on, you can do it!"

I straightened out my black-and-blue suit, stood up straight and tall, and took a deep breath. My split leap wouldn't be perfect. In fact, it would be pretty awful. But these were my friends. And it was a beautiful summer day that I wanted to remember forever. So, like I'd done lots of times that summer, I told fear to sit down and be quiet.

And then I ran.

And I leaped.

And for one brief moment, it felt a little bit like I was flying.

Friends
A poem by Lindy Mackay

Someday
I'll look back at this day,
with the sun on our cheeks
and the wind at our backs,
and I'll think, "That was a great day."
But it's not the ocean
or the sky or the sand
I'll remember most.
It's how you made me feel.
Happy.
Safe.
Loved.